His eyebrows flew up.
"You're a what?"

Dani puffed out her cheeks and expelled a breath
of exasperation. He was looking at her as if
she had sprouted two heads. She reached inside
her pocket for her badge and whipped it out,
letting it dangle about a foot from his nose.
"Danielle Sweet, HSA Intelligence, federal agent."

But Ben Michaels was already shaking his
head. "That's pretty damn convenient." Then he
squinted at her. "So you were already on to this
guy, and led him into my bank, endangering my
employees?"

She laughed bitterly. "Oh, yeah, I was on to him
the *instant* he stuck his gun into my back in your
bank's doorway."

**Start off the New Year right—
with four heart-pounding romances from
Silhouette Intimate Moments!**

Lyn Stone

SPECIAL AGENT'S
SEDUCTION

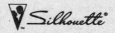

INTIMATE MOMENTS™

Published by Silhouette Books

America's Publisher of Contemporary Romance

For fellow traveler, research assistant and ski-buddy, Al.
Thanks again for sharing life's adventures!

 **SILHOUETTE BOOKS**

ISBN-13: 978-0-373-27519-9
ISBN-10:   0-373-27519-6

SPECIAL AGENT'S SEDUCTION

Visit Silhouette Books at www.eHarlequin.com

Printed in U.S.A.

Books by Lyn Stone

Silhouette Intimate Moments

Beauty and the Badge #952
Live-In Lover #1055
A Royal Murder #1172
In Harm's Way #1193
Down to the Wire #1281
Against the Wall #1295
Under the Gun #1330
From Mission to Marriage #1444

*Special Ops

LYN STONE

loves creating pictures with words. Paints, too. Her love affair with writing and art began in the third grade when she won a school-wide contest for her colorful poster for Book Week. She spent the money on books, one of which was *Little Women*. She rewrote the ending so that Jo marries her childhood sweetheart. That's because Lyn had a childhood sweetheart herself and wanted to marry him when she grew up. She did. And now she is living her "happily ever after" in north Alabama with the same guy. She and Allen have traveled the world, had two children, four grandchildren and experienced some wild adventures along the way.

Whether writing romantic historicals or contemporary fiction, Lyn insists on including elements of humor, mystery and danger. Perhaps because that other book she purchased all those years ago was a *Nancy Drew*.

Dear Reader,

Imagine a bank robber accidentally grabbing a federal agent to hold as hostage! Impossible? Nope. Agents bank like everyone else does.

The real-life incident that sparked this idea was told to me by my hubby and his cohorts and took place in Korea. It seems a rather clueless entrepreneur chose the wrong place to recruit new drug customers. He waltzed right into the unmarked building housing CID agents and Military Intelligence personnel and made his pitch. Caught unaware, the agents actually played along until one could get to his badge and weapon and arrest the guy.

No one in that instance suffered any real threat, other than laughing themselves to death. But I wondered what would happen if there were a serious one-on-one situation and the only weapon was in the hands of the criminal.

No similarities in the two events? Right you are. Sparks and tangents. Such is the convoluted way books are born. Now you know how a fiction writer's mind works.

I hope you enjoy the sparks flying! Two control freaks on a mission together equals instant conflict. Toss in a desperate physical attraction they dare not admit to and bring on villains who show no mercy.

Enjoy the op!

Lyn Stone

Chapter 1

"Feel the gun?"

Danielle Sweet froze in the doorway.

Earlier that morning the old familiar feeling of unease had shot up her spine. She *would* pick today to ignore it. She had figured, "what could happen here in lazy old Ellerton, Safety City itself?" Well, hey, now she knew.

But even now, caught in the act of pushing open the bank door with a gunman behind her, the feeling didn't seem quite sharp enough to warrant panic. She could handle this. More than fear, she felt anger at herself for having lowered her alert level.

Assess the threat. Make a plan.

This man behind her had parked next to her, greeted her as she got out of her car, and asked politely if it was nine o'clock yet. She had sensed him walking nearby as they reached the portico of the small Beresford First National Bank.

He looked to be in his early thirties, weighed around two hundred, moved with confidence, no hesitancy. He spoke with a slight accent, looked professional, unremarkable. Even with their contact she hadn't thought much about him at first.

At least he wasn't some scruffy, unpredictable druggie hell-bent on grabbing some fast cash and ending it with a killing spree. There had been no flashes of imminent bloodshed along with the niggling little premonition she had shoved aside earlier. Of course, that might or might not be reliable.

The pistol prodded her spine. She imagined she could feel the roundness of the barrel right through her coat. "Go in. Smile," he ordered. "Act normal. Behave as though we are a couple, if you wish to survive."

Okay, *survive* was a good word. As soon as they entered the front door, he halted. "Remove your coat," he ordered.

Dani shrugged out of it when he released her arm. Hurriedly, she tugged off her gloves to free her hands for combat if that became necessary.

She would have already risked taking him down

if it were just the two of them, but there were others in the bank. Better wait to see how it played out. He immediately clutched her again, his ungloved fingers and thumb biting painfully into her bicep.

Her service revolver lay locked in her briefcase in the trunk of her car for the duration of her visit with her sister. There was nothing she could do at the moment but comply and silently curse the fact that she was unarmed.

She had decided to stop at the local bank to set up a savings account for her brand-new nephew and present the parents with it as one of her baby gifts. The decision, almost a compulsion, had been with her since she'd woken up this morning: insure that baby's future. God, she wished she'd bought the little fellow a teddy bear instead.

But maybe it was better that she had come here. Maybe she'd been meant to be in the bank for this.

The barrel of the weapon nudged her again and she heard the man's satisfied grunt. No wonder he was pleased. There were only three other people inside.

One young woman was humming along with the soft lobby music while she worked on the bins of deposit slips, forms and pamphlets at the counter in the middle of the room. A teller, Dani guessed.

A skinny, older man of around sixty lounged in the doorway to one of the two glass-fronted offices within the lobby. He wore a mud-brown off-the-rack suit and black patent shoes. Not exactly the type who would be meeting the public much. She would guess accountant. He chatted with a younger man who stood propped against the desk. Now this one looked the part. They were both sipping from coffee cups. Smiling. Shooting the breeze.

In a small town like Ellerton, Virginia, even with traffic severely curtailed by ice and snow, surely there ought to be more people minding the store. Of course, anyone with good sense would be home today, snuggled by their fires. The streets were a mess. The guy had chosen the perfect time for a bank heist.

She shifted position and even tucked her shoulders in a little, hoping the hand that clutched her arm would ease its grip.

"Interfere and I will shoot you first," her captor whispered. He squeezed her arm harder, hugging her closer as he led her farther into the lobby.

The blonde turned to them, smiling. "Good morning. What can we do for y'all?" The men across the room continued talking, drinking their coffee, offering only a cursory glance.

Suddenly a hard twisting motion almost cracked the bone in Dani's arm. She cried out sharply, trying to jerk away, but the pain nearly sent her to her knees.

She sagged against him to keep from falling. She dropped her coat and purse.

At her cry, the men rushed out of the office to see

what had happened and the blonde hurried over ahead of them.

The man's gun hand flew up, the weapon near the side of Dani's face. "Stop! Move and she dies."

They stopped in their tracks, all three now within six feet of Dani and the man who held her, well away from any alarm buttons. That was the point to the distraction, she figured.

She looked up at the bank employees, expecting expressions of shock. Only the younger man showed none. No fear, either. His glare rivaled the ice on the streets outside. He looked seriously ticked off.

Don't be a hero, she prayed.

For a minute, Hero looked like he might give it a shot. He and the perp were about the same size, both over six feet tall, both built like they worked out religiously. If not for the gun, a 9 mm holding fifteen rounds, they would probably be pretty evenly matched.

Dani had to let the scene unfold without attempting to interfere, and she hoped the banker had come to the same conclusion. She could take the gunman by surprise and probably disarm him, but the situation called for prudence. She wasn't the only one at risk here, and above all, she didn't want anyone hurt. The money was insured. Bank robbers got caught.

She glanced up and could plainly see two cameras. There would be a couple more stationed somewhere behind her. This entire escapade would be recorded, so knowing what the perp looked like didn't put them at further risk. There was no reason for him to kill them if they kept calm.

"Where's the vault?" he demanded.

The older man pointed to the hallway around and behind the counters.

"Go there. All of you. Single file," he demanded.

Whew, he was just going to lock them up, Dani thought with relief. They would sack up some money for him and he'd simply lock them inside and leave. A few hours later they would be watching his arrest on the evening news.

He snapped out another order. "You and you, go inside!" He motioned with the weapon for the older man and the girl to enter the vault. "Lock the door," he said to the younger guy.

The girl began to wail and plead like a four-year-old. The sound cut off the instant the thick steel door clicked shut. At least this narrowed the list of potential casualties. Those two should be safe enough.

Dani's arm throbbed, still caught in a viselike grip.

"Back into your office," the robber instructed. "Remain on the front side of your desk."

She met Hero's gaze and raised her eyebrows. He was red in the face, his strong jaw and fists clenched.

Don't try anything! Dani tried to communicate the thought to him without words. He shot her an exasperated look, exhaled sharply, then turned with military precision and led the way. Message received, she guessed.

When they reached the office, the robber forced her into the chair to the side of the desk, he stood behind her, placing the muzzle of the gun to her right temple.

"You. Stand," he ordered the banker. His accent became more pronounced and his breathing grew more rapid. "Keep both of your hands in my sight at all times. No silent alarms or she dies. First, turn the monitor around so that I can see it clearly. Move the keyboard to this side," he demanded. The hero eyed him, but complied.

"Now, send this fax," he instructed the man, placing a document on the desk. "Be certain to dial correctly." Dani watched the process as closely as her captor did.

When the fax machine whirred, the perp tossed an index card down in front of the keyboard. "In the left column there are account numbers. From these accounts, I wish the amounts listed in the middle column transferred to the account on the right."

"To the Caymans?" Dani heard a barely concealed scoff in his voice.

"Begin."

"I need the code to access the program used for transfers of this nature," the banker insisted. "It's in the vault."

"You know the codes," the robber growled. "I kept

you out of the vault because you are the manager. Do it now or she dies. Then you die. Make no mistakes."

The banker's lips firmed. Dani watched the muscles in his jaw clench while he did as he was told.

This took a while since there were quite a few transactions involved. From her view of the monitor, Dani noted that none of the amounts were too enormous. She didn't bother to keep a running total, but figured it at around three million.

The robber picked up the notes. "I wish to see confirmation when it is complete."

The banker paused to await one of the steps of the transfer to go through. "I see you've kept the amounts under a hundred thousand, but the transfers will send up red flags anyway."

"I know," the robber said, an evil smile in his voice. "But these will be *your* red flags."

Survival seemed a lot less likely now, Dani thought with a belated surge of adrenaline. There was something in the man's voice and movements, a subtle, higher pitch, an increased tension and a slight tremor in the hand holding the gun. He was building up to something, getting himself psyched.

She remained motionless except for her gaze, which settled immediately on an engraved name plate that read Benjamin R. Michaels. The name suited him. Strong, no-nonsense, bankerly.

Dani watched the banker's long, tapered fingers

fly over the keyboard and listened to the soft whir of the computer as it completed its functions. Meanwhile, she smelled the sweaty wool and scent of anxiety that cloaked her captor.

The cold metal of the pistol brushed against her hairline, sending chills down her spine. All her senses edged to higher alert levels. She could taste his fear like metal on her tongue. Now this man would have to kill them both. They had seen the numbers. If he let Michaels live, the transfer could be reversed, or at the very least, reported in detail. If not reported by any survivors, the transferred funds could be moved again from the Caymans and disappear.

Dani squeezed her eyes shut and a chaotic picture flashed through her mind, a Technicolor explosion of action, a split-second portent of extreme violence. This was no flight of fearful imagination, but a bona fide premonition.

Late warning. Maybe too late. She had to *do* something.

She blinked fiercely to clear her head. The bank manager's steely gaze met hers as they waited for a response from the target bank. He knew, too, that they would have to die. And Dani realized if she didn't try something in the next few minutes, this would-be hero *would*.

Even as she tried to formulate a less risky plan, her right hand slid slowly up her body, past her breast, so that her fingers barely touched her collarbone. The robber's attention stayed on the screen. As if reading her mind, Michaels tilted the screen a little more to the right, providing distraction.

Striking like a coiled rattler, Dani's hand shot up, grabbed the robber's wrist and shoved the pistol up and away from her head. Several rounds hit the wall to her right. She dug her nails into the nerve at his wrist, felt her nails cut flesh and saw the gun tumble onto the desk.

A backhanded blow knocked her completely out of the chair and slammed her against the wall. Even while she scrambled upright, she focused on the struggle between Michaels and the robber as they fought for the weapon.

Again, it discharged, shattering the tempered-glass window.

More shots! Chaos! The scene that had flashed through her head earlier morphed to reality. Adrenaline surged and gave her strength.

Desperate, Dani attacked from the rear. She leaped onto the robber's back and clutched her legs around his hips. She dug her fingers into his face, trying to gouge his eyes, anything to disable him. But her hands slid all over his skin, sticky and wet. To her shock, he crumpled to the floor beneath her and lay still.

For a long moment she couldn't move. Straddling the perpetrator, her hands still locked around his head, she waited for him to recover and resume fighting.

"It's over. He's dead," a calm, deep voice assured her.

Large hands slid beneath her arms and lifted her off the body. Before his words could register, he had turned her around and embraced her, holding her close, pressing her face to the soft cotton of his shirt. His subtle cologne mixed with the tinny smell of blood.

She pushed herself away from the admittedly warm embrace.

"Thanks, but I'm okay," she stated, but the words came out a little shaky and breathless, not as firmly as she meant them to. "Are you?"

"I'm fine. Why don't you go in the other office and sit down while I call the police?" he suggested.

"Check the body," she ordered. "Just to be—"

"Sure," he said, finishing her sentence and turning her toward the door, his strong arm locked around her shoulders. "Trust me, he's dead. Come on now, let's get you out of here."

Dani broke away. "Hey, I'm not falling apart, Mr. Michaels, and I don't need any babying. I'm a *federal agent* and I can handle a little blood, okay? And rule number one—I check to see if the perp is dead or not."

His eyebrows flew up. "You're a *what?*"

Dani puffed out her cheeks and expelled a breath of exasperation. He was looking at her as if she had sprouted two heads. She reached in her pocket for her credentials folder and whipped it out, letting her badge dangle about a foot from his nose. "Danielle Sweet, Homeland Security Intelligence."

But he was already shaking his head in obvious disbelief. "That's pretty damn convenient!" Then he squinted at her. "So you were on to this guy? And you led him into *my* bank? You endangered the lives of *my* employees?"

"Oh yeah, I was on to him the *instant* he stuck his gun in my back. And since we were already at the front door, your bank just seemed like a great place to get the goods on him, so I brought him on in!"

The sudden silence seemed deafening. She suddenly realized just how loudly she'd been screaming at him.

Chapter 2

Dani tried to calm down and contain the shakes. Her whole body seemed to vibrate uncontrollably now that the threat was over.

"What were you doing here in the first place?" Michaels demanded.

Dani rolled her eyes. "Hey! *Banking,* maybe? Am I allowed?"

"You don't have an account here!"

She threw up her hands, clenched her fists and turned away so she wouldn't smack him. After a few deep breaths, she faced him again, measuring her words, moderating them into a somewhat mocking semblance of normalcy. Man, she needed some normalcy right now. "I came to open one!"

Defuse this right now, she ordered herself. Say something nice. Another deep breath. He was pacing now, his stride severely limited by the floor space available. "By the way, thank you for not doing something too stupid and getting us killed."

A muscle worked in his jaw, clenching, unclenching. He stopped pacing and glared at her, his eyes flashing. "*Stupid?* You mean like grabbing somebody with a gun pointed at your head? Like leaping on his back? Stupid like that? Dammit, he could have taken your head off, you know that? Of all the freakin', idiotic—"

"Shut *up!*" Dani snapped. "He was about to kill us both anyway and you knew it! So don't you rail at me for—"

"Okay, okay!" he interrupted, struggling with his temper. A moment later he had his palms out in a gesture of surrender. "Let's let it go. It's over and we're both alive. Just calm down, all right?"

"I'm *calm* as a *cucumber,* Slick. *You're* the one going ape. Now, why don't you do something constructive like get the hell out of my way?"

His intense gaze remained on hers as his breathing evened out. He jerked one hand toward the dead man. "Be my guest, then. Check the body while I notify the police."

"Fine," she snapped. "*Do* that."

Ignoring him, Dani crouched beside the dead man and felt his carotid for a pulse. Then she saw why he said it wasn't necessary. There was a bullet hole right between the eyes, which were open and already glazing over. Plus, he had a massive exit wound at the top of his head.

If she hadn't been so much shorter, she would have seen it when she'd jumped him. With that thought, she suddenly realized her hands were gummy. She examined them and began to worry about contamination from the blood.

"Bathroom's that way. Better go wash that off," Michaels said, pointing. He had gone around to the other side of his desk and stood waiting with the phone to his ear.

His perfect features held an expression of worry now. New frown lines forming. Probably his first serious problem, she thought. Men who looked the way he did must have a really easy skate through life. A hiccup like this was enough to throw him off polite behavior.

Dani felt bad about their heated exchange. Adrenaline could do weird tricks with a person's attitude. Unfortunately, it seemed to have affected them both the same way. She would need to apologize later.

In the meantime, she retrieved her purse from the

lobby floor, hurried to the restroom where she scrubbed off the blood. Thankfully, she had no scratches to worry about. Her right temple felt completely numb where the pistol had been jammed against it, though that was probably due to swelling from the blow she took. Her hip hurt where she had crunched it against the wall and her arm ached a little. Otherwise, she was okay.

Carol was going to kill her. It seemed every time Dani got within a mile of her sister, trouble exploded. Last visit, Bud's new car had been stolen out of their driveway and found burned to a crisp over in the next county. Dani, a brand-new agent working for the Bureau then, had felt obliged to hunt down the guys who took it and bust up the car-theft ring. Bad call, jurisdictionally, she remembered. This time, she'd stay out of it and let the locals do their worst.

Even when she and her sister were growing up, Dani had been a trouble magnet. She was invariably swept up in the middle of whatever conflict developed anywhere near her, mostly due to her acting on her dratted premonitions. Maybe she had cursed them once too often. Today her Gypsy mother's gift of foresight had all but failed.

Or had it? Maybe it had taken a different form with that pressing need to get out of the house on a day when sane people stayed inside. And that sudden notion of opening an account for the baby had struck her like a hammer just after breakfast. Had that fore-sight guided her here to stop the robbery?

Maybe she shouldn't have come to Ellerton in the first place, but how could she stay away when Carol had a brand-new baby, Dani's very first nephew? It wasn't as if she was likely to have any children of her own any time soon, maybe ever.

Once again, she reminded herself why she had no business envying her sister the adorable baby, devoted hubby and the white picket fence. Mommies weren't supposed to carry weapons and go looking for danger, like she did for a living. Like she enjoyed doing. It was not a life to be shared with innocents.

But what if she hadn't come? Ben Michaels would probably be dead right now, as well as whomever else the robber would have held hostage instead of her.

She glanced in the mirror again, examined the new bruise on her head and pulled some of her bangs down to cover it. *Out of sight, out of mind:* one of those sayings that didn't quite work in this case. Later, she'd cover it with makeup, but it would still ache like crazy.

To distract herself, she thought about Michaels as she made herself presentable. It took a certain kind of person to settle down in Smallville and be content. Someone like her sister and Bud, her brother-in-law. And this Benjamin Michaels, big bad bank manager. He had been unexpectedly cool under fire.

The thought made her wrinkle her nose. Hero material, sucked into life as a bean counter. How the devil had that happened? She pushed away from the sink and went back outside. Maybe she would ask him.

He stood near the front door, waiting for the police. From some back office, probably the employees' lounge, she could hear the blond teller weeping dramatically and the other guy mumbling.

She crossed the lobby to Michaels. "So, could you reverse the transfer and get the money back?"

"No. I—" Sirens and the screech of tires interrupted. The police hadn't had far to come. You could span the whole town in about five minutes.

The small bank filled with people. Three uniforms, six emergency personnel and a couple of plainclothes carrying satchels, probably doctors or crime scene techs. Who would guess there were this many people in Ellerton to respond to a call like this? It was comforting to see, given that her sister and her family lived here.

A pleasant-looking, heavyset man in a cheap suit entered and approached them. He removed his hat, revealing a silvery crew cut and a tan line on his high forehead. His bright blue eyes snapped with energy. She recognized him immediately and cringed.

"Hey, Ben," the police chief said, glancing in the direction of the office where the paramedics were hovering. "Everybody okay?"

"Everybody but *him*," Michaels said, gesturing idly toward the body.

The chief looked at her, head cocked to one side. "Miss, I'm Chief Talbert with the Ellerton police." He cleared his throat and squinted. "Don't I know you?"

Dani shrugged and tried to look innocent.

The chief's eyes narrowed farther. "I need to interview y'all separately. Ben, you want to scram? I know you got things you need to do, calls to make and so forth, and we can talk later."

"I do at that." Turning to her, he said, "I'll see you later. I'd like to speak with you again before you go."

Dani nodded. His low-timbre voice had a newscaster quality to it, softened by a distinct Virginia accent. Nice, she thought. Exceptionally nice, when he wasn't cussing or threatening. *That* tone matched his polished appearance.

Amazing, how unruffled he looked now. The only evidence of the altercation were his skinned knuckles and minute spatters of blood on his shirt. The man obviously had a tough side, one he masked well. Dani consciously made note of the fact that it was a really good-looking mask. No wrinkles, not even any laugh lines. Smooth. Almost mannequin smooth. She wondered if he was vain enough to be into Botox.

Her budding fascination must have shown as her gaze followed him, because the chief cleared his throat yet again, this time to get her attention.

Dani ignored him for another few seconds as she watched Michaels head for the other unoccupied office. She liked the way he moved, how he led with his left, leaned forward and swung one arm in a John Wayne kind of stride. But the Duke on his best day had never looked that good. She allowed herself a silent little *whew* before she looked away.

"Okay, here you go." She reached into her pocket, fished out her badge folder and handed it over.

The chief took it and examined it closely. "Uh-huh. So you're a special agent, division of Homeland Security." His smile looked wary. "Wait a minute. Weren't you with the FBI?" She saw recognition dawn. "I remember you now. Whatcha doing here in Ellerton this time, Ms. Sweet?"

"On vacation." *Again,* she thought, but didn't add the word. "Visiting my sister, Carol Whitman."

Surprisingly, his smile turned friendly. "She and Bud had the baby yet?"

"A boy." Dani went on to explain why she was at the bank and gave him the details of what had happened. Then, just to be polite, she added, "Can I be of help other than as a witness? If I can assist in the investigation in any way…"

He smirked a little, obviously recalling the last time their paths had crossed and how she had stolen his thunder. "No thanks, I think we can handle this one. So you're with the COMPASS outfit now? We got some directives down a couple months ago about cooperation and interaction and such. Part of that special team, Sextant, aren't you? Counterterrorism?"

"Yes, we're an adjunct to Sextant." She smiled. "Look, Chief, could you maybe keep my name out of things? I'd consider it a big favor. We like to keep a low profile."

He nodded. "Sure thing. Okay, that about does it. Thanks."

Dani followed him over to the door of the office where the EMTs were bagging the body.

"Well, Ben took care of *him*." He sighed and rubbed a hand over his face. "Pretty cut-and-dried, I guess. Bank job gone bad. I need to go question Ben and the others. Maybe you should stick around until I'm finished, in case I come up with any more questions. You mind?"

"Glad to," she replied, in no great hurry to face her disapproving sister with the news of her latest adventure.

A little while later, Ben Michaels returned to the lobby. He managed a more pleasant expression than any he had shown before. She registered again how perfect he looked. Short dark hair expertly cut. Nice, smoothly arched brows. Steely gray eyes rimmed with long black lashes. Lips that really made her pause to stare. Nose every plastic surgeon must aim to duplicate. Cheekbones that hinted at Native

American genes beneath his pale skin. Except for a few hairline scars, nothing marred the mask. How benign he looked now. Great camouflage. She almost said so out loud.

"I shouldn't have popped off at you the way I did," he said. Perfect Southern gent routine, smooth as good cane syrup. One would never guess he had a pop-off in him.

"Not a problem," she said, sort of aping his accent, simply because she liked it. Her natural Midwestern clip seemed a little blunt by comparison. "Guess I did the same thing. We were both pretty wound up."

He either didn't notice or ignored her Scarlett O'Hara impression as he nodded and inhaled deeply, releasing it slowly before speaking again. "Could I talk with you in private about what happened?"

Well, that raised her brows. "What for?"

"You're Homeland Security and I have a possible threat to discuss."

"Does it have to do with the robbery?"

He nodded. Dani decided to humor him. He had been through a lot this morning. He would naturally blow this all out of proportion—she had seen it many times. A thief, obviously of foreign extraction, had come in to rob the bank, to direct the funds out of the U.S. Had to be an international plot, right? Small towns were a refuge for foreign professionals. Her sister's obstetrician was from India. All the convenience stores were run by recent immigrants, as were many of the mom-and-pop motels. This guy looked like a well-to-do businessman in his expensive top-coat and tasteful tie. Some immigrants were office workers, some blue collar, and, yes, some were thieves. But not all of them were linked to international terrorism.

Amid these doubting thoughts she became very aware of Ben Michaels's hand on her elbow, guiding her to one of the empty offices even before she had noticed. At least he wasn't causing any premonitions of danger. She smiled at the thought.

"Okay, Mr. Michaels, explain this potential threat," she said in her most authoritative tone.

"Please, make yourself comfortable." He gestured for her to sit in one of the wing-backed chairs that flanked the desk. Then he closed the door and sat across from her in the matching chair. Through the plate glass that separated the space from the lobby, Dani could see the beehive of activity as the locals went about their investigation.

She waited for him to begin. He searched her face, assessed it, as if trying to determine something about her.

She studied his, too, along with his body language and general demeanor, all of which signified his great concern, but also evident was his confidence to deal with whatever may trouble him. He certainly had done all right so far today, no question about that.

He seemed to reach a decision. "We might have a terrorist funding situation going on here that your people should investigate. At least you can pass it on to the agency that handles such things to see if I could be right."

"Even foreign nationals commit regular crimes, Mr. Michaels. They're not all sleeper agents committed to a holy war. And for all we know right now, this guy's a U.S. citizen, born and bred. Bank robberies are not in my bailiwick."

He leaned forward, his hands clasped between his knees and his penetrating gray gaze holding hers. "I realize that, Ms. Sweet, but this wasn't your run-of-the-mill robbery," he said, stating the obvious. "I was forced to dump three million from legitimate accounts here into the bank in the Caymans. It was supposed to appear as if *I* had done it. Embezzlement."

"I got that," she said wryly, inclining her head in agreement. "Are you saying this type of robbery has never happened before in the annals of bank heists?"

"Cute. What I'm saying is that these funds may have been taken from the accounts of individuals who share a common cause. Individuals who might not mind their accounts being victimized."

"Say it straight-out if you don't mind. What's the deal?"

"I said it already. Could be terrorist financing."

Dani cocked her head and stared at him. "What are the chances of that? A terrorist stumbles in here and inadvertently takes an intel agent hostage?"

He shrugged again. "That's the reason I asked why you were here."

"Okay, exactly *what* do you think is going on? Paint me a scenario."

"Say he left no witnesses. Then he goes to the back of the counter to the drawers and takes all the cash he can carry and gets away. This would have been considered a straight robbery. Later when the auditors come in, they discover the transfers I've made to this offshore account. I probably would have been blamed for it." His gaze was keen, sharp. "Didn't it seem to you as if he *intended* for me to take the heat? You remember, when I mentioned the red flags?"

Dani didn't quite buy it. "The time would have been recorded as happening during the robbery," she reminded him.

"Yes, but this audit would happen weeks later. The money trail would end at a Cayman bank and they would never recover the funds."

"The cameras would show you performing the transaction under duress."

He glanced out at the cameras. "We haven't gone digital yet. Easy to remove the evidence with no one alive to stop him. Granted, it doesn't seem like it was a great plan on his part, but he and the money would have disappeared before anyone sorted it out. And if I were missing, I would definitely be suspected of collusion."

"I think your supposition is a stretch, Mr. Michaels," she said, although she privately wondered…Michaels was no alarmist. He seemed cool and collected and had obviously given this a lot of thought.

"I'm not through yet," he stated, his tone flat and unequivocal. "You need to listen to me and have this checked out." He gestured emphatically with his hands as he spoke.

He continued to lean toward her, his palms flared as his elbows rested on his knees. "The money is insured, so the clients wouldn't have suffered any loss."

"I'm listening," she told him. "Please go on."

He met her gaze, sincerely trying to convince her of his theory. "Today's crime could have played out the way I suggest if we hadn't stopped it. Your basic robbery, then later on, an unrelated incident of embezzlement is discovered. The apparent perpetrator of that, namely me, already dead. Or maybe he would have forced me to go with him, only to kill me later."

Dani leaned back in her chair. "Why your bank?"

"Maybe we have all the right customers. The upshot is that I think the funds I was forced to transfer could have already been earmarked to finance terrorists."

"Three million would only be a drop in the bucket to those groups. Maybe our guy was merely a thief who didn't realize the Cayman banks are not a good place to hide funds anymore."

"Oh, I think he knew he couldn't hide it there. He only needed to get it out of the States first." Michaels abandoned his ingratiating pose, sat back and crossed his arms. "You won't find the money there anymore," he told her with absolute authority.

"Why are you so certain of that, Mr. Michaels? Have you already moved it? Did I happen along at the wrong time and mess up a little plan to cover up a three mil heist with a simple bag job?"

Chapter 3

Michaels didn't bat an eye at her accusation. "I am trying to help here. If the robber and I were in cahoots, all he had to do was lock you in the safe, too. Or kill you outright."

In cahoots? Dani stifled a smile and nodded, tongue in cheek. She didn't really suspect Michaels of involvement and he knew it. "I still think it's quite a stretch, bank robbery to terrorism. Are you deducing all this from the robber's physical characteristics?" She had to admit, though, that the thought had crossed *her* mind when she first felt the gun and heard the accent. But that was a panic response, not good inductive policework.

"Not entirely."

"Okay, let's explore the possibility." She encouraged him to go on. His certainty was a little contagious. "Explain why else you would think he was a terrorist collecting funds from sympathizers?" she asked.

"While you were talking to the chief, I checked the numbers of the source accounts against the surnames of the holders. Those names reflect that this could be an effort by individuals with possible familial ties to the Middle East to amass a tidy sum, jump it from country to country and land the funds where they could easily be accessed as needed."

"*All* of the account holders? There must have been thirty accounts you drew from."

"In total, there were only nine individuals and companies. All have multiple accounts with us and all of those accounts were tapped. All except one have ties to the Middle East, or at least surnames that indicate they might. One of the smaller accounts has a name very similar to an organization on the terrorist watch list," he said.

Dani dropped any pretense of disagreement. He had made his case, or at least enough of one to warrant a full investigation. "I'll notify the agency. They'll institute a thorough investigation. You can't recover the funds? Have you tried?"

He rolled his eyes. "Of course I tried. Part of it was withdrawn within seconds of the transfer, and most of it was transferred again. It stands to reason there would be an accomplice waiting at the other bank to move on it quickly. It was split. Looks like the man at the other end took his cut." He paused. "But I can follow the money they moved."

"You can do that?" she asked. "How?"

"Well, shift funds around all you want, but it always leaves a trail. As you probably know, there's really no such thing as an anonymous account anymore. I have connections that could furnish names and leads to follow. It's a place to start."

Dani recognized competence when she saw it. "My people can call on the Mutual Legal Assistance Treaty the offshore banks signed with the UK and the U.S."

For the first time, he smiled. "That would help. As you pointed out, a few million's not much in the grand scheme of things. But if you multiply it by a number of small banks like this one, terrorists could secure an absolute fortune before anyone recognized what they were doing." He shrugged. "Or I could be wrong. This could be a setup to ruin me and my bank."

"You have enemies who would do that?" she asked, almost smiling at the thought. He appeared so benign, so likable. "Look, no one believes you were involved in this. Insurance will take care of the losses. Why not let it go at that?"

"You're kidding, right? Let it go?"

"You seem to be taking it very personally," she said, wondering how far he'd work this theory of his.

He planted a fist in his palm and bared his teeth in a grimace of frustration. "Of course I do. This bank is my responsibility and my reputation was threatened."

After a pause, she said, "Okay, let's word this for my boss so I can run it by him and I'll make a call." She poised her pen over the little notebook she always carried in her pocket. Michaels cleared his throat and began. He dictated clear, concise sentences, like Dani had read in many official government incident reports. Dani noted the way his dark gray eyes narrowed as he drew to a close. "If those funds are meant to support terrorists, we need to make sure that doesn't happen. I mean to make certain it doesn't."

His last sentence brought back some doubt to her. Was he a glory seeker trying to get his name in the papers by making up some fictitious plot? All the agencies got scads of those. So many they were now having to prosecute the "witnesses" when fraudulent intent was clear. False claims tied up too many people in useless investigations and took time away from real cases.

Or did Michaels really have something? It was never wise to consider any citizen's suspicions frivolous, no matter how outrageous they sounded. And, unfortunately, his sounded feasible.

"What if this was just a little more sophisticated than your everyday bank job?" she suggested. "Our boy probably knew all the tricks about tracing stolen money when a thief actually carries it out in a sack, like the dye, the tracking devices, marked bills and so forth. Crooks *do* watch a lot of television."

He acknowledged with a wry smile. "Add to that the fact that few banks actually keep three million in cash lying around. And even if we did, extremely large bills are too hard to spend without raising questions. And a cache of small ones in that amount would be too damned heavy for one thief to carry."

He dropped the smile and looked away. "Besides, I haven't mentioned the clincher, the thing that convinced me this was no regular heist. Make sure *this* is in your notes."

Dani turned the page in her notepad and clicked her pen.

Michaels met her gaze with one of pure fire. "He muttered something immediately after the transfer, just before you acted. Did you hear it?"

"Sounded like a curse," she replied. "To tell you the truth, I was too busy concentrating on what I was doing."

"It was a phrase in Arabic," Michaels told her. "He said *Death to America*. Then the rat bastard smiled."

* * *

Dani's eyes widened and she sat silently for a moment. "You speak Arabic, Mr. Michaels?" Now this seemed a lot less far-fetched than it had before.

He shrugged. "That particular phrase is one I heard enough times to engrave it on my brain."

She leaned forward. "And just what did you do in the service?"

If he was surprised that she had guessed he was former military, he didn't flinch. His beautifully sculpted lips tightened into a line before he relaxed them. He promptly reverted to the stillness that signified his stolid banker image before he replied. "I picked up phrases like that one."

"Ah. Okay," she said, clicking her pen rhythmically, watching his eyes. "Did you mention your theory to the chief?"

"No, it's not within local scope. That's why I wanted to speak to you about it."

She nodded her approval. "Could you step out and give me a few minutes to make a call?"

He stood, then paused before leaving the room. "Just so you know, I plan to follow through on this. Nobody…I mean, *nobody,* rips off *my* bank and gets away with it. Especially not for the purpose of bank-rolling the bin Ladens of the world. I can track the money." He shook a finger at her. "You tell your people that. They can work with me or around me, I don't really care—but there's no way I'll be camping out behind some desk while someone else tries to straighten this out."

Whoa. The man didn't come off like a mild-mannered banker when he got his dander up. But Dani knew what her boss would say to having a civilian muddying up the waters of an international financial investigation. "We have experts who follow up on things like this, Mr. Michaels."

"And by the time they decide who and how many to send, get the travel approved, orders cut, run everything through their computers and bureaucrats, and settle on what to do first, the money will be spent. And if I'm right, people will die."

The fire in his eyes told her he'd had some experience with that. She could also see that her words would have little effect on his actions. Plus, he was right about the systemic delays. That was one reason her own team had been formed.

Whoever investigated this would certainly need the cooperation of a banking expert, and Ben Michaels did have all the particulars of the transaction and perhaps knew how to trace it, if that were possible. She would at least call the boss to see what he thought about Michaels, his suspicions and his plans to pursue this. Maybe the investigating operatives could use him.

"How are you with team work?" she asked, suspecting that he might have a lone wolf personality.

"Depends on the team," he replied. "But I can work alone." He paused, again with that narrow-eyed glare that hinted at hidden hard edges and left Dani assured of his resolve. "And I *will* if need be."

Dani took out her cell phone and raised her chin to indicate he should leave her to make her phone call in private.

"Ben Michaels, you are one lucky son of a gun," Mike Talbert said with a roll of his eyes. "Guess you been living right lately."

"Has Mary Ruth calmed down yet?" Ben asked, changing the subject. He was concerned about the young, newly hired teller who had thrown up all over the inside of the vault and fainted. Her every waking moment since this whole thing started, she had spent crying. She looked about the same age as Agent Sweet. He couldn't help comparing the two women and wondered what had forged Sweet's ironclad nerves.

"Aw, Mary Ruth'll be okay," Mike said. "Probably need some counseling, though. Doc gave her a little something to take the edge off and I sent for her daddy to come get her."

"And George?"

"He's fine. Gave us the details on what happened right up until the vault clicked shut on him." Mike smiled. "George is good with details. Prob'ly already writing a book about it."

Ben tried to smile back.

"Where's our little agent?" Mike asked, then peeked around Ben's shoulder. "Oh, there she is. This COMPASS team she's on? I've heard of it through channels. Started out as one of those secret, specialized forces called Sextant, which has branched out to include this new one."

"Not so secret now?" Ben asked.

"Publicly, they are, but in law-enforcement circles they're growing their legend. See, they took the best of the best, so I've heard, from the Bureau, CIA, NSA, ATF and the like. Supposed to stimulate cooperation between the agencies. Must be working because that first bunch has made quite an impact, heading terrorists off at the pass. COMPASS was involved in some real dicey deals with stolen missiles, bombs and such."

He nodded toward the office and smiled. "Hard to believe Miss Sweet's up to things like that, the way she looks and all. Kinda dainty."

Ben clicked his tongue. "You didn't see her disarm the robber. She's gutsy. And quick."

"Like a bunny," Mike said, laughing. "Yeah, she whipped our asses on a car theft thing here a couple of years ago. Made us look like a buncha yokels. It was all over before we even knew what was going on…. I ought to be mad at her for that, but I never been one to hold a grudge. Besides, she's a real looker."

A real looker. "And *you're* a real master of understatement," Ben said with a laugh. Agent Sweet was a natural beauty with a perfect, tawny complexion, clear amber eyes and rich dark hair so shiny it reflected her red sweater. She filled that out magnificently, even though he doubted she weighed much over a hundred and ten pounds. A five-five bundle of energy with a good head on her shoulders. The view from the rear in those gray slacks impressed him, too, as she turned her back on them, still talking on the phone.

Too bad she'd turned, though, because those mobile lips of hers were her best feature, Ben decided. God, they were something.

"She might be good at what she does, but you're the one who was really on the ball today, man." He slapped Ben on the shoulder. "You sure you're okay? Still look a little tense."

"I'm fine and I'd appreciate it if you'd downplay my part in this," Ben replied, his gaze still focused on Agent Sweet.

"Oh, 'cause of your mama, right?"

"Right." He watched Agent Sweet pace behind the glass window of the office. She gestured emphatically with one hand as she talked into the phone.

He wondered if he would see her again after today. He hoped not, he reminded himself firmly. There was already one woman in his life he had been jumping through hoops to keep happy for the last year and a half.

All that aside, nothing prevented him from enjoying Agent Sweet aesthetically. She was a work of art, that one. Through the window her dark golden eyes met his and locked like lasers. Then with a curt motion of her hand, she beckoned him to join her.

Even her frown was intriguing.

Despite finally being able to leave the scene, Dani felt anything but relief when they exited the stifling bank into the cold air. Vacation was over. Mercier had decided she should follow up on this since she was already familiar with the situation. And, surprisingly, her boss had not discouraged Michaels's involvement, at least as far as the Cayman bank.

She could feel one of her premonitions coming on and this one felt like a doozy.

Everything had happened so fast. Capable as Ben Michaels had seemed in the crunch today, she did not want to work with a civilian, even if he was a former soldier. She had only the bare bones of his career; Mercier had run a quick check on him, then read her the high points over the phone, assuring her Michaels was qualified to act as an agent of opportunity.

Michaels had been out of the army for almost two years after serving for seven, an officer nearly halfway to retirement, now a bank manager. Medical discharge, Mercier said. Probably high blood pressure, Dani figured.

"Follow me," Michaels ordered as he reached his vehicle, a fairly new Mercedes SUV sporting snow chains. The boy must make pretty good money, Dani thought.

"We'll go to your sister's house to drop your car. Since I have chains, we'll take mine from there. My dad can drive us to the airport."

Mercier was arranging for their tickets to Grand Cayman. Even though the account there was closed out now, she'd been ordered to collect any surveillance tapes or paperwork that might be important, conduct some interviews and back up Michaels in his attempts to collect info on where the money went. *Back up.* Ugh.

He was already trying to take charge, but Dani decided to pick her battles—no point sweating the small stuff. This type of op was new to her, so she *would* have to follow his lead in some respects. But she was in charge and he needed to understand that. If it had to do with anything other than locating that money, he would damn well have to do what *she* said.

"Bud could drive us to the airport," she offered, a little reluctant to offer the services of her brother-in-law when he had a new baby at home to help care for.

"We'll see. It depends on how my mother reacts to the news that I'm leaving," he replied.

Dani frowned as she slid into her rented sedan and slammed the door. It sounded very much like she might be dealing with a mama's boy. One of her few forays into relationship territory had pitted her against a proprietary mother turned tigress. What a disaster that had been. Soon as Mama had found out about Dani's Gypsy roots, she'd started applying weed killer.

Funny, Dani would never have figured Ben Michaels for a guy who hung on the apron strings. Showed how clueless she still was about men. Too bad her famous premonitions didn't extend to pro-filing. Her gust of frustration produced visible vapors in the freezing air. Oh well, it was nothing to her. She wasn't interested in him *that* way.

Still, the little frisson of disappointment wouldn't go away. Maybe she was a bit more interested than she wanted to admit. With more force than necessary, she twisted the key in the ignition, jerked into Reverse and backed out of her parking space.

If Mama said he couldn't go, Dani would just leave him the hell at home. Not as if she needed to play nursemaid to a damn banker anyway.

Mercier had agreed the banker's assessment of the terrorist funding deserved checking out. More manpower would be on it shortly, he had assured her. She was to get a jumpstart by going to the Cay-man bank and hopefully getting a lead on whoever had been there in person.

Mercier had spoken on the phone with Michaels

at some length and decided the former army officer ought to lend his expertise in banking operations and contacts in the field to Dani's investigation, at least to the preliminary portion of it.

When Dani turned into the driveway at Bud and Carol's house, Michaels pulled up behind her and got out. He had her door open before she even had her seat belt unlatched. "Mind if I come in with you? I haven't had a chance to congratulate them on the baby. Bud's an old friend."

So he knew Bud. She wished there were time to grill her brother-in-law for the local skinny on Michaels. "Sure," she said, slipping a little when she stood on the icy cement.

He clamped an arm around her waist. "Careful there."

Dani didn't jerk away from him. She knew she should have, would have automatically, as a rule, but there was no point risking a fall. And, to tell the truth, she didn't mind a bit that Bud saw the embrace through the window where he was watching them approach the porch. He was always teasing her about her badge putting men off, but Dani figured he was just worried that she would influence Carol to be more independent. Men could be so insecure.

Bud met them at the door. "Are you all right, Dani? Ben? I just heard the bank was robbed! Come on in and sit down!"

Now she felt guilty for her sniping thoughts about Bud. He really did love her like a sister, and he had a big brother attitude. "Where's Carol? We need to talk."

When her sister appeared, Dani wasted no time relating what had gone on at the bank. Ignoring Carol's worried frown, Dani laid out her plans to leave while Michaels sat quietly next to her on the sofa. "Ben has agreed to assist with tracking the stolen funds, so he'll be coming with me."

"I can *not* believe this," Carol said, rolling her eyes. "What is it with you, Dani? Every single time you show up…"

"Not *every* time!" Dani argued pleadingly. She sensed that she and Carol were about to take up their age-old conflict again and wished she could avoid it. The visit, up until now, had gone so incredibly well.

For two women whose features were so much alike, they were polar opposites otherwise. Carol the peace lover, versus Danielle the daredevil. They had gone through life that way.

"I'll take you to catch your plane, Ben," Bud declared. "Your dad's gonna have his hands full." He shook his head at the thought.

Michaels declined. "Thanks, but I've actually decided to drive us and leave my car at the airport."

Dani exchanged a look with Carol, who had obviously decided not to fuss anymore. Her sister merely raised her eyebrows and gave Dani a tight-lipped grimace.

"Let me say goodbye to our Little Buddy first," Dani said, heading for the nursery. "I won't be but a minute."

"I'd like to see him, too, if it's okay," she heard Michaels say. She sensed him follow her down the hall.

The baby slept, his tiny rosebud of a mouth slightly open, the multicolored knit cap slightly askew on his bald head.

Dani couldn't resist picking him up. Her maternal instincts fired up again as she held the sweet-smelling bundle against her chest, enjoying the waking squirm, the mew of protest at his nap being disturbed.

She laughed softly and whispered, "No rest for the weary, huh? You be a good boy while I'm gone and Aunt Dani will bring you a surprise when I come back." She swayed gently, soothing him back to sleep. "Bye, sweetie." She placed him back in the crib, touching the soft blanket with her fingers in a last caress.

Michaels stood beside her, looking down with something that read like yearning. "I always forget how small they are when they're brand new."

She smiled up at him. He had not mentioned a wife or children. There had only been a photo of an older couple in his office, probably his parents. "You have any kids of your own?"

"No, no children." His words were slow, some-how sad.

"This one's a little miracle, isn't he?"

Michaels nodded, his gaze fastened on Buddy. "A new life. Always a miracle."

Dani left him standing there in the nursery, hands clasped behind him and looking at the baby. As she went to pack what she needed for the trip, two questions bugged her. Did he want children all that much? And, why should she care?

Chapter 4

A half hour later they reached his house—a gorgeous Victorian that belonged on a Christmas card. It was especially lovely dressed in its light coat of snow. Carol and Bud's bungalow looked like a dollhouse by comparison.

"Maybe I should wait in the car," she said. If he expected a scene with his mother, Dani definitely did not want to be witness to it—she'd seen enough ugliness today.

"Of course not. There's always coffee on and we can grab a bite to eat before we go." He got out and hurried around to open her door for her.

She still felt reluctant to go in. Though his words were sincere and hospitable, she caught the undertone of dread in them. What did he expect, a spanking or time-out in his room? At any rate, this little episode might well extinguish any looks-based romantic notions possibly forming in her subconscious.

They navigated the slick stone steps, which someone had dutifully sprinkled with what looked like kitty litter to combat the ice. She admired the front door with its beveled panes and oak frame. "Your house is beautiful."

He scrubbed his shoes over the rough mat. "It's my parents' place, but I live here, too. And you might as well call me Ben. I'll use Danielle, if you don't mind. My calling you 'Sweet' could get awkward."

Dani nearly laughed. Yeah, she'd bet Mama wouldn't cotton to that worth a damn. "It's Dani for short."

He walked right in without knocking, which was appropriate, she reminded herself, since he *lived* here. A grown man who lived with his parents. Déjà vu all over again.

"Benjamin!" a thready voice cried from the room on the right. A wispy woman of around sixty appeared in the doorway, arms outstretched. Her eyes were red and puffy, and she carried a wadded tissue in her hand. "We've just heard what happened at the bank. They interrupted programming on television with the news. Are you all right, son?"

"Fine, Mother. Nothing to worry about." He embraced the woman, who had her eyes squeezed shut, tears running down her cheeks as she hugged him hard.

Her voice rose nearly an octave. "What's happened to you? I can tell when something's happened." The woman grew even shakier, trembling like a frightened bird. She seemed to notice Dani for the first time then. "Who is this?"

Dani froze the smile on her face, determined to keep it there even if things got ugly. If life went true to form, the agent in the house was about to take the heat for involving favorite son in an upcoming op.

Ben stepped back, carefully taking his mother's hand in his. "This is Danielle Sweet. She's a government agent and just happened to be at the bank today. Danielle, my mother, Martha Michaels."

"Nice to meet you," Dani said with a small nod as she fought the bizarre urge to curtsy. She didn't figure the woman would go for a handshake at this point. Maybe at any point.

Ben cleared his throat, obviously uncomfortable. "Let's go sit down and I'll tell you everything. Where's Dad?"

"Here," answered the tall, silver-haired gentleman striding down the central hall. "I was in the den listening to the latest about the robbery. You'll have to give us the straight of it, though. Those news people tend to exaggerate."

Not this time, she'd bet, thought Dani. If Ben Michaels did have the straight of it, things were much worse than the media realized.

After her introduction to his father, they went into the living room. Dani took a seat on the Victorian sofa at Ben's indication. He waited until his parents were seated in the matching chairs that faced her, then sat beside her.

In a carefully modulated voice, he gave a seriously watered-down version of what had happened at the bank, leaving out any reference to his struggle for the weapon or the fact that he shot the perp. "Danielle very skillfully brought down the man who robbed us," he said finally, and gave her a beatific smile. "We're very lucky she was there today."

"You saved my boy?" Mr. Michaels asked, giving her a quizzical look. His expression said he didn't buy that scenario for a hot second. The mother was looking at her with something approaching horror, but whether it was on Dani's account or Ben's, it was hard to judge.

Dani glanced at Ben for direction. He just looked at her blankly. "Well…it's all in a day's work, sir." There. She gave a little shrug.

Ben looked away and studied the window for a minute, watching it snow. Then he dropped the bomb.

"I need to pack a few things. Danielle and I are going to the Caymans to make some inquiries about the stolen funds."

"No!" His mother shot up out of her chair, exhibiting sudden agility for one who appeared so frail. "You are *not* getting yourself mixed up in this. It could be dangerous!" Her face crumpled a little and her voice rose and broke. "Benji, you...promised me."

Benji? Oh, boy, bet you love that nickname, Dani thought, biting her lip and trying not to smile.

Ben was there in a heartbeat, his arms around the woman, one hand patting the head she had nestled on his chest. "The danger's past, Mother. The man is dead now. No threat at all."

"There could be others working with him," his mother argued, her words muffled against his chest.

So Mama wasn't clueless. Dani wondered if Mrs. Michaels had noticed the few specks of blood on her son's dress shirt. Dutiful son would have changed that shirt if he had seen them himself. Maybe he was a little more distracted than he appeared.

He set his mother away from him, still holding her shoulders gently. "You shouldn't worry, Mom. I'll be perfectly safe and be back home in a few days."

Dani started to speak up to tell his parents that he wouldn't encounter any risk. Michaels had said the money was gone from the Cayman bank now. The only purpose for going there was to get information about the person who had shown up to collect part of it and transfer the rest. Interviewing bank employees presented no danger. But she decided to keep her mouth shut and let Ben handle his folks.

His father took over the support role and gestured with a jerk of his head for Ben to go and pack. Hesitantly, Ben did, leaving Dani to witness the older couple's silent struggle and the mother's tears.

"I think I'll just go wait in the car," Dani muttered, and headed for the door. "Nice to have met you both."

"Wait, don't do that," Mr. Michaels said. "You'll freeze out there. Why don't you go to the kitchen and have some coffee?" He pointed the way. "Just make yourself at home."

Dani gladly left the room, following her nose to the coffee. Adrenaline rushes ate up calories faster than any workout. She was starving and hoped Ben's offer of a quick meal would hold up, even if she had to watch him placate his mom's fears while they ate.

She found a mug and helped herself to the brew. Taking Mr. Michaels at his word, she made herself right at home and raided the cookie jar. She munched rather contentedly as she leaned against the counter and waited.

Within ten minutes Ben reappeared with a travel bag. He had changed out of his suit into cords, a brown pullover and boots.

"How L.L. Bean," she remarked, grinning up at

him over her cup. Her hormones revved like a souped-up Harley. Ben Michaels was a hunk, no doubt about it. She raised her mug. "Coffee?"

He wore a steady nonexpression. Great poker face. Great face, period. But unless he wanted you to know what he was thinking, you never would guess.

"Let's go," he said.

She was ready, full of the pilfered chocolate-chip cookies and not at all averse to hitting the road. But in spite of his words, Michaels seemed fairly reluctant to travel. "Aren't you going to say goodbye to your parents?"

"I did. It's snowing harder. If we don't leave soon, we might not get a flight out."

Goodness, he sounded almost hopeful. Mommy must have read him the riot act or hit him with another dose of guilt. At least he hadn't caved completely and told Dani to go on to Grand Cayman by herself, as she had half expected to happen.

She shrugged and set her cup in the sink. Maybe she shouldn't judge him so harshly. So what if he lived at home and was under Mama's thumb? Maybe he needed his folks. Maybe his experiences in the service had caused a bad case of posttraumatic stress or something.

Dani doubted that, though. When it came down to performing in a life-or-death situation, he had proved himself more than capable. No hesitation and apparently, no bad aftereffects. She could work with him. And so she promised herself she would not get personally involved with this guy, no matter how he physically cranked her tractor. One trip down *that* road was quite enough. After that one, she had decided her next boyfriend would be an orphan with no mother around to mess things up. She had held to that decision, but, as it happened, her second relationship had turned out even worse than the first. Her luck with men was awful.

When Ben took her arm going down the steps outside, Dani pulled away. She marched across the icy yard and opened her own car door. Self-sufficiency had become her credo these last few years. She had leaned on her last man and sure as heck didn't want one leaning on her.

Ben wondered what had set her off. Her sudden pique annoyed him. Maybe she resented his coming along on her mission. Well, that was just too bad. She could just deal with it.

"Messy day all around, isn't it?" he asked as he got in and buckled up.

"The rest of it certainly was, but I love the snow," she stated. Her tone was defensive, even argumentative.

"Me, too," he admitted. He recalled having dreamed about it while traipsing across burning desert sands and crawling through scrubby hills in

Afghanistan. He liked drifts of snow four feet deep, covering everything with its pristine whiteness.

He felt a sense of urgency mixed with dread that he had not felt for nearly two years. But *that* threat had been up close and personal. It had been immediate. This one could have far-reaching effects across the world.

His world had already blown up once, a private disaster, nothing as earth-shaking as a globe vulnerable to terrorists.

Maybe he was wrong about the robbery. He sure hoped so.

He pinched the bridge of his nose then ran a hand over his face. Strange how it still felt as though it belonged to someone else. The nerves and muscles were obviously working. He could smile, frown, whistle, raise his brows. But the nose was wrong, too straight. The cheekbones, a bit high. Whenever he looked in the mirror, he wondered how much of his character had disappeared with his real face.

The surgeons had done a bang-up rebuild and he had nothing to complain about. It was better than having no face at all, which was pretty much where he had been eighteen months ago. They had given him the closest thing to a face transplant possible without actually using someone else's tissue. A total transformation. A miracle, really.

The only thing that looked remotely like the old Ben Michaels was his eye color and the line of his jaw. He had to deal with the strange new mug and get on with his life. Up to now, he thought he had been adjusting really well.

Today's events had held up a mirror he hadn't looked into before. With the new face, he had taken on a new personality and a new job. Now Ben saw very clearly that his life had become all pretense. A necessary pretense, he reminded himself, one he had to embrace.

He would get back to his new life soon, but first he had to do this. No point in doing it halfway, either.

"Want me to drive?"

Ben jerked out of his reverie and glanced over at the woman. "No, I'm good."

"No doubt. Did you bring a weapon?"

He dipped his chin in a nod. "Beretta. Packed it in my bag. I have the paperwork on it."

"You need a Walther PPK."

"Sez you."

She laughed, but it sounded odd. "You know what? I couldn't bring myself to pack mine away. It's in my purse and I'm clutching it like a security blanket. I called my boss and had him make arrangements for me to carry it on the plane. Is that a hoot? This morning's events must have struck a little deeper than I first realized." She sighed. "I was kicking myself the whole time for not having it on me when I needed it. Now since I won't let go of it, I'm stuck with marshal duty for the flight."

Ben understood about the gun. When he was in the hospital, blind as a bat and knowing he was surrounded by caring people, he still reached for that holster if something woke him from a sound sleep. The weapon hadn't been there, of course, but he had still reached. Habits died hard. They could die, though. "You'll get over it," he told her.

"I know I will," she agreed. Then she took a deep breath and turned sideways to face him. "Ben, do you really want to do this? I have the feeling you've got some major reservations about it, even though you volunteered."

"Nope, I'm in," he assured her without even looking over, shaking his head for emphasis. "No reservations whatsoever."

What a bald-faced lie. But it was not fear of danger that stifled his enthusiasm. Not fear for himself, anyway. And not for Danielle Sweet, either. But if he ended up dead or wounded again, he knew his mother might not survive this time. He worried about her more than he could say, but she wasn't the only one he had to consider here.

If he thought this money eventually helped finance even one act of terror and he hadn't done all he could to prevent it, he could never live with himself.

"Tell me how you got on to this team of yours," he suggested. That should fill his mind with something other than its current dark thoughts.

"When I was with the FBI, I shot a CIA agent," she replied, securing his full attention. He nearly ran off the road.

"I'm sure *that* endeared you to everyone in the Bureau. Did they promote you immediately?" He managed a grin. "You *are* joking, right?"

She shook her head, pulling her dark hair to one side and twisting the silky ends.

"He had turned," Ben guessed.

"Yes." She didn't elaborate.

Her sadness permeated the car and he could damn near feel her hurt. "You were involved with him," he guessed again, thinking that nothing else could cause that sudden expression of grief. Taking any man's life could cause terrible regret, but the effect on her seemed to cut deeper.

"It came down to him or me and my partner. Let's let it go at that."

"No problem." His hands tightened on the wheel and he squinted into the distance ahead.

She hadn't meant to share that episode in her life, he figured, and was not about to elaborate on the circumstances to a virtual stranger.

Ben tamped down his curiosity, cursing his need to reassure her that she had done the right thing. Surely she knew that already. But that knowledge could not simply erase all her feelings about the lover she had shot.

Seeking something pleasant, neutral and not to do with jobs, he asked, "So, where are you from?" keeping his voice light.

"Iowa," she replied curtly and without a hint of affection for her home state. He had never been there and knew nothing about it except that corn grew there. Maybe she had been glad to leave.

"Your folks still there?" he asked.

"No." Then a cold silence.

"Just trying to make conversation," he said.

She didn't answer. Two strikes and he was not going to swing again, but he couldn't help wonder why she was so stingy with personal information. He tried to recall what he knew about her sister, Carol, but nothing came to mind. Bud had never mentioned Carol's family, not even that Carol *had* a sister.

The sisters looked enough alike to be twins, although he sensed a profound difference between them. Carol's hair and complexion were a shade lighter. Her eyes were pale brown instead of Danielle's rich, dark amber. But there was a more marked distinction. Carol cast a warm steady glow about her. Danielle shot hot sparks in all directions. They almost couldn't be more different.

Neither Ben nor Dani spoke again until they reached the airport. There, everything was all-business as they glided through security on her badge and credentials and boarded the plane for Grand Cayman.

She sat in back, out of his sight. Ben settled down in his seat just behind the wing, reflecting on how odd he felt without her next to him. How the devil could he miss her company when he barely even knew her?

And yet he had seen her quiet and cautious under threat of death. Definitely well-trained and level-headed. He had seen her attack with every ounce of her strength. Certainly courageous and aggressive. And he had seen her with a baby in her arms. Soft and maternal. How did those qualities combine and emerge so fluidly in a matter of hours? Somehow they did and the process fascinated him. It made him wonder what other qualities he might discover as he got to know her better.

No doubt facing and cheating death together caused a bond of sorts to form. He had seen it happen before. It had happened to him, so he also recognized how superficial that bond could be over the long term. He made a conscious decision not to delve any further than necessary into Danielle's psyche. He couldn't afford to get entangled with anyone, not with his life as it was now.

Besides, her job would take her away from him the minute this mission was over anyway. He would go back to banking, living out his promise to his mother. Dani would chase terrorists or do whatever else the government put in her job description. Their little twain wasn't likely to meet again. Which might well be for the best.

He shifted restlessly, grimly accepting that his size would not allow comfort in tourist class seats and stared out the window into the darkness. Ben saw that he was naturally drawn to her because she represented everything he had been forced to leave behind. But the strength of his heady attraction to her didn't diminish at all with that realization.

It didn't seem right that he was looking forward to these next few days, but he was. She was his ticket to visit that world he had lost.

Chapter 5

"You have reservations for Danielle Sweet," she said to the desk clerk. The hotel was a modest, mid-priced accommodation near the bank instead of one of the resorts on the beach.

"Yes, here it is," the clerk answered. "Two rooms, singles, for the remainder of tonight and tomorrow night."

"Right." Dani plopped down an agency credit card and pushed it across the desk with one finger. She flashed the young man a winning smile.

"Adjoining?" the clerk asked pleasantly.

"We *will* need to confer, so that would be convenient," Ben said, wondering if he had lost what marbles he had left. He probably wouldn't sleep a wink with her in the next room.

She signed the form and took the key cards without offering an objection. They followed the bellman to the elevators and up to the second floor. There, they parted company and went to their respective rooms to settle in.

Ben opened the case with his laptop and hooked it to the available connection. He checked his weapon, loaded it and put it in the drawer beside his bed.

It had to be eighty degrees in the room in spite of the air-conditioning. He shed his shirt, sweater and shoes and was wearing only his cords when he heard a knock on the connecting door.

"Forget something?" he asked, opening the door slightly.

"I just talked with Mercier." She shouldered in past him.

"Come right on in," he offered a little sarcastically, and followed her to the sitting area with its pair of chairs and round table. "So, what's up?"

She scooped his shirt off the chair and tossed it onto the bed, then plopped down, pen and little notebook in hand. "Okay, you said you had contacts? Who are they?"

"Jim Fontenot. Friend of a friend. Bank security."

He looked her over, noting she had changed into

lightweight drawstring pants and a yellow ribbed tank top. Her hair was caught up in an off-center ponytail and trailed down over one ear. She was barefoot. And braless.

He figured Dani had either borrowed some of her sister's summer clothing when she packed her bag or else was always prepared to visit any climate whenever she left home.

Though she looked fresh as spring itself, her eyes indicated exhaustion. Still, she was probably too keyed up to sleep after all that had happened. "Are you hungry?"

"I'm absolutely starved, and I forgot to ask about room service. You think they deliver this late?" It was nearly midnight.

Ben picked up the phone. "Breakfast okay?"

"Perfect. Get the works if they'll do it."

"But with decaf," he remarked. "Can't have you hyperactive. God knows you're energetic enough without that."

She laughed. "You have no idea. Even in the best of times, I tend to bounce off walls. Have you spoken with anyone lately about establishing off-shore accounts?"

There was no segue there. If she had hoped to catch him off guard, she had. He put the receiver down. "What do you mean?"

"Just that. Have you had any conversation that involved talk of accounts offshore?"

He thought about it and couldn't recall anything specific. Then it came to him. "Yeah, I think. It was, oh, several months ago at the gym. A guy asked me in passing how hard it was to set something like that up. The main gist of the exchange concerned my warning him that it was not a great way to try to bypass the IRS, if that was what he had in mind. He laughed a lot at that, maybe a little too much. I never gave him any real particulars about doing it, though, just general stuff."

"You remember his name? Where he was from?"

Ben shook his head. "Not anyone I knew, just some guy. New in town, he said. We were working out. He asked what I did for a living, then launched into all these questions. I thought he was just lonely, didn't think much about it."

She jotted down a few notes then looked up. "You were working out? How was he dressed?"

Ben frowned. "What?"

"Could he have been wired?"

"How the hell should I know? What's this about?"

She sighed and clicked her pen rhythmically. "Chief Talbert found a tape in the glove compartment of the robber's vehicle. It was a tape of you and another man making plans to establish offshore accounts." She paused. "For making funds available for foreign projects."

Ben was already shaking his head. "No. *No way* did we discuss anything of that kind. I'm telling you it was just an offhand Q and A. I thought he had watched too many movies and I told him so. This guy was thinking to get out of paying his taxes, that's all."

She sat back, abandoning her note-taking and stretching her arms above her head, obviously unaware of the picture she made doing that. The sight made him sweat bullets.

"Don't worry," she said. "The tape was doctored. Even Talbert picked up on that after he played it the second time. Background noise was different where they inserted your voice, volume was a little off where they spliced it. Answers didn't quite match up with the questions, that sort of thing." She smiled at him. "Your cop buddy was ready to go to the mat for you when he reported it. He thinks a lot of you."

Ben took several deep breaths to relax. He knew then that he'd been suppressing his natural reactions for too long. It hadn't been all that difficult at first when all his energy had gone into his recovery. Easy to believe he'd had enough excitement in his life, enough adventure to settle down. To become like his dad.

The robbery had put a definite crack in his resolve to be who he needed to be. He hadn't really changed the way he thought he had. Maybe a man couldn't alter who he was, how he thought and responded— or maybe he just had to try harder.

He would do that, he promised himself. But not until this was over.

He did tamp down his anger at Danielle, however. She was only doing her job. He forced a wry smile. "Thank God they weren't more proficient. What if they had matched the splicing better? You'd be arresting me for collaboration."

Her succinct nod didn't make him feel any better. "Somebody wants you tied to this, Ben. They went to a lot of trouble to see to it that you are."

"Who? What good would that do?"

She sat forward and clasped her hands together over her notes, flicking the corner of the tablet with one finger. "That's the question, isn't it? Guess we'll have to dig around and find out. Mercier's sending us a copy of the tape to see if you recognize the voice, but it's a good bet it was the guy you remember from the gym setting you up."

For a few minutes neither of them spoke.

She broke the silence first. "What about that food?"

Ben ordered, then took the chair across from her to wait for it. He leaned back and crossed his arms over his chest. There was no point obsessing about who had it in for him until he had more information. "Maybe this *is* a personal vendetta against me and nothing to do with terrorists. That would be a relief, wouldn't it?"

"Definitely the best-case scenario." She gave a

one-shouldered shrug and grinned. "But let's not assume anything this early in the game."

His laptop issued a soft ding, alerting him that his download on the potential contact, Fontenot, was complete.

"E-mail from home?" she asked.

"Not yet. Just doing a little homework." He brushed beads of sweat off his forehead. Her presence wasn't helping. "Hot in here, isn't it?"

"Yeah." She fanned her neck with her hand, obviously a bit nervous now that she found herself in the room with a half-dressed man in the wee hours of the morning. Instead of trying to put her at ease, Ben simply waited to see what she would do next.

"Stop looking at me that way," she said with a half laugh, tucking her hair behind her ear in a self-conscious gesture.

"What way is that?" he asked.

"Like you're afraid I came in here to...well, maybe come on to you or something."

Ben pursed his lips and inclined his head as if thinking about that. Actually, he was thinking about it, or at least considering whether *she* had thought about it before she knocked on his door.

"I'm not all *that* afraid."

She laughed outright, a beautiful uninhibited sound he hadn't heard before from her. Like music. "You're teasing me, Michaels."

"No joke," he said, shaking his head. "I could take you. You really don't scare me a bit."

She sobered as she rose from the chair, slid open the balcony door, stood in the opening and looked out at the sea. "Even after admitting I shot a man?"

Trying to still make light of the mood before it became irrevocably serious, he said, "Even so. If you recall, I shot one, too."

Many more than the one today, actually, but he didn't want to get into that now. Or ever, if he could avoid it. He felt himself growing serious.

Ben wanted to know her, he realized. He felt driven to for some odd reason. Her beauty played into it, sure, and her strength of purpose, but he thought it must be her passion for life that drew him to her, probably because he had spent the last year denying his own.

There was something else about her. He sensed a streak of vulnerability in Danielle that he suspected few ever witnessed. Not physical defenselessness, but emotional.

There were family issues with her, he knew that. Didn't they *all* have those? She refused to discuss her parents, her background in Iowa or anything to do with her past. Someone had hurt her badly enough to silence her. That agent, maybe. The one she took down. He must have meant a lot to her. Maybe to her family, too.

Ben wished they were well enough acquainted

that he could insist on knowing, and not just to assuage his curiosity, either. He wanted to listen and maybe help her deal with whatever caused the bitterness he sensed beneath that tough little exterior.

Or maybe he should just mind his own business. He had to watch his strong impulse to protect. It had cost him his life already. And resurrections were probably a one-time thing.

In spite of the best intentions, Ben got up and stood behind her. He raised his hands to her shoulders and turned her around to face him. He ran his palms up and down her bare arms, knowing it was a mistake.

Not a serious mistake, he assured himself. She needed human contact, a friendly touch, comfort. The memory of holding her immediately after the shooting surfaced. "You're still shaken up by this morning, aren't you?"

"Yeah, a little," she confessed, leaning back against the door frame as she looked up at him. Her hands rested lightly on his arms, as if they were already close friends consoling one another. "Maybe since you were a soldier once you know how it is."

"Tell me how it is." He gently dug the pads of his thumbs into her muscles, rotating, easing her, which did excite him a bit, but he wanted to keep his mind on helping her.

She drew in a breath and released it slowly before she explained. "Well, when you are expecting something to go down, you get yourself psyched up for it and have all your contingency plans made and everything. You're armed, have backup, a Plan B in case Plan A goes south."

He nodded.

She shook her head slowly. "But then you're relaxed, not psyched and then—bam!—some nut sticks a gun to your head while you're busy thinking about babies and gifts. It's unnerving."

He smiled down at her. "I was having my first cup of coffee of the day. He caught me while my nerves were still asleep."

"Guess that explains why you didn't get all hysterical, huh?"

"The only reason. Lack of caffeine," he said, letting her go before he gave in to the urge to lean down and kiss her. That, even in his warped attempt to justify touching her, could not be considered mere comfort. He stepped away so she was out of his reach and sensed her disappointment. It mirrored his own, but neither of them could afford this distraction.

"Better get back to business," he said. "We'll see Fontenot first thing in the morning and find out what he can get for us."

"You just happen to know a guy who works at the very bank the money went to? That seems coincidental." Ben caught the suspicion glowing in her amber eyes just before she lowered her lashes.

"I don't know him personally. I got into the bank's Web site and accessed their personnel listing, got his name and had my contacts search his background. You'd be amazed at how many security people are former military."

"You hacked into the bank?"

Ben shrugged. "I needed names."

She raised her eyebrows, but didn't question his hacking any further. "Is he from your old outfit?"

"No, but we know some of the same people." Intelligence was a brotherhood of sorts. Ben didn't want to get into all that at the moment. He had signed that nondisclosure agreement and, even though she was intel herself, he firmly believed in need-to-know dispersal of information. "Anyway, I talked to Fontenot on the phone and set up a time for us to see him."

Her smooth brow furrowed as she looked up. "I don't think we'll have the authorization from OFAC that soon."

"The Office of Foreign Assets Control? Maybe we won't need it."

"It *would* slow us down if we have to wait for it," she said with a sigh.

Ben shrugged. "I'm pretty sure Fontenot will cooperate fully, but anything he can't readily access might necessitate going through other channels."

She flicked a glance at his laptop. "You said you can follow the money. By hacking?"

"How smart would it be to admit a talent like that to a government agent?"

She trained her gaze on the ceiling. "I could say something about the end justifying the means, but I won't."

"Thank you for that, at least. And to answer your question, I don't make a habit of it."

"Make a habit of it now," she demanded, leaning forward. "Let's see what you can do." Her hand landed just above her left breast. "My oath, I won't report you unless you steal something or wreck a bunch of files." She smiled. "And I'm sure you'll tell me if you do that."

"I'll let you watch. What do you want me to try?" As he spoke, he sat in front of the computer.

She tapped her bottom lip with one finger. "Who do you think is behind this? Any suspects?"

It was his turn to ruminate, or at least to pretend to. Any number of outfits could be organizing this effort, but one had leaped to mind the minute he made those transfers. "How about the largest client involved, the one that has no apparent ties to anything Middle Eastern?"

"Isn't that one more likely to be a victim?"

He shrugged. "Makes you wonder why it was included, doesn't it? If that particular outfit screamed theft immediately, it could blow the whole plan. Assuming I'm right about the plan."

"Okay, that makes sense to me. Go for it. Check out that client's computer system," she said, taking the other chair and nudging his laptop so she could see the screen, too.

He pulled up the company Web site, checked it out, then began his real search.

"You plan to get me out of hot water if I get caught snooping?" he asked as he activated the exceptional password program he used and waited for it to unlock the site. "If they have crack security, they'll know they've been invaded."

Her frown deepened. "What about the bank you hacked? Won't they know, too?"

"I covered that. Their system's set up almost exactly like mine except for the extra safeguards I added."

He couldn't help noticing as she leaned in closer, affording him a glimpse of cleavage when she peered at the screen. The warm scent of her clouded his brain. He shifted nearer so that her breath fanned his cheek.

She quickly sat back, averting her gaze. One hand slid up to her chest and flattened the neckline of her top. "Just don't damage any of their files. Breached privacy issues I can probably justify, but not data altering."

Ben closed his eyes and tried to think of anything else but her. He opened them again and zeroed in on the screen where the password box blinked, waiting for an entry. The code locator program scrambled some letters by the cursor and entered a string of letters. The bank computer readily accepted the entry. "We will be fishing with a big net. What if we happen to catch something incriminating that has nothing to do with our case?"

"I don't know. Go ahead," she said, motioning with her fingers for him to continue. "You're not a fed, so this is not technically a *government* search, just a nosy attempt by a private citizen trying to recover his bank's money."

Ben stretched his arms, flexed his fingers, made an adjustment to the program and smiled at getting past the first of what would probably be many obstacles in the mystery. "This could take a while."

"I'm not going anywhere," she replied, propping one foot on the edge of her seat and hooking her hands around her knee. "Go ahead and show off, cybergeek."

He didn't see the harm in flirting with her a little. Nothing serious, of course. Why *not* try to establish a little camaraderie?

"Ah, here we go. This is the Persand Company," he said as he reached the page delineating the victim company's executive officers.

"What?" she asked, glancing from him to the screen and back again. "What did you find?"

Ben said nothing. He felt light-headed and sick at his stomach. Wordlessly, he pointed to the name that had immediately caught his eye before he'd even scrolled down the list. It was there on the third line, bold type, underlined for a link to more info.

"*You?*" she whispered. "You're the operations manager?"

"Hell, no!" he exclaimed quietly. He clicked on his name and another page appeared with his photo, the one from his bank business card, and a very short résumé that looked quite convincing. "I've never had any dealings with Persand Inc., except through the bank."

He navigated back to see who else was listed under executive officers. Slowly he nodded, his lips tight with fury.

Dani wasn't looking. Her chin propped on steepled fingers, she seemed lost in thought. Then she spoke. "Well, you wouldn't have pointed it out to me unless you were telling the truth. Someone is definitely setting you up. I need to tell Mercier about this."

Ben couldn't hide his relief. She did believe him. He just wondered if everyone else would.

"Let me dig a little further."

Room service came and Dani busied herself with the food as he worked. She brought him a cup of coffee and put his plate beside the computer.

He had made it to Persand's financial data. He ran the password program again and ate as he waited. Dani remained silent, alternately watching him with his silent posture and the screen with its chaotic text crunching.

"Pay dirt."

"What did you get? What *is* that?"

"It's a private file that was labeled *Beresbnk*. Close enough to Beresford bank. Tabbed columns. Looks like a list of names, account numbers and amounts. In simple code, but the keystrokes and spaces are right. See? Same format as the robber handed me in the bank, only the letters and numbers are coded." He downloaded the file to his desktop. "Should be easy to decipher."

"This links Persand to the robbery," she said, wriggling in her chair, lifting her other foot to the chair and clasping her hands together around both legs.

"If it's what we think it is," he replied.

"It has to be," she said, sounding nearly as desperate as he felt.

Rain beat down on Victor Bruegel's roof as Miami suffered an unusual winter deluge. A boom of thunder woke him from a sound sleep in time to hear the subtle purr of his phone.

He cursed and sat up. Victor hated interruptions of any sort, especially when he was sleeping. He felt he had earned the right to uninterrupted rest.

Angrily he reached over and punched the speaker phone button. "This better be an emergency," he snapped, plowing his fingers roughly through his thick curly hair and massaging his scalp. Increased barometric pressure made his head ache.

"It is, sir. The company computer system has been violated. Not the usual attempts, but someone searching for information."

Victor sighed. "Do something about it then. That's what I pay you for, Terrence. Trace whoever it is and find out what they're after." He coughed. "And make sure they don't get it!"

He could hear Terrence swallow hard before answering. "We traced the hacker, sir, and actually found his location. I don't think he was trying all that hard to cover his tracks. It's like he wanted us to know."

"Well?"

"The hacker is at a hotel on Grand Cayman. The computer is registered to Benjamin Michaels, manager of the Beresford bank in Ellerton, Virginia."

The bank job in Ellerton had obviously failed. He had known that was a distinct possibility and planned for it. Still, he rolled his eyes and cursed again. God, Michaels must lead a charmed life. He was supposed to be dead by now. Even the memory of him was to be reduced to smut. Damn him!

Terrence continued, unaware of his announcement's full impact. "The room at the Cayman Hibiscus Hotel where he is located now is in the name of Danielle Sweet." There was a significant pause before Terrence added, "She used a government issued credit card."

Victor hadn't expected the feds to move this

quickly, though he had counted on their getting involved in the investigation. In the course of that, Persand would be involved, but only as a target of theft. Victor had even planned to let the feds dig around a little. Just far enough to find Ben Michaels's name on the org chart in just the right place. "How far in did he get?"

Terrence didn't answer nearly as quickly as Victor would have liked. "Pretty deep, sir. He breached payroll and employee information."

Not good if Michaels was doing the hacking and had noticed a Benjamin Michaels there. He might guess he was being set up. But even if that happened, he would have trouble convincing the feds that he didn't own a piece of the company. And it would be doubly obvious that he was involved since he would have to admit having access to the company information. Yes, this could work to the advantage.

Terrence was still talking. "The hacker entered your peripheral files, too. Of course, you have everything there well coded. What are your orders?"

Victor had frozen in place, his bare toes digging into the plushness of the carpet as he sat on the edge of the bed. This was *not* good.

"Find and dispose of Michaels immediately," he said, trying to sound calmer than he felt. "Also anyone with him and any individual who received a transmission from him, electronic or telephonic. Understand?"

"You wish Mr. Kelior informed?"

"Immediately. *All* resources on this, Terrence. It's crucial we kill this investigation and everyone associated with it. Move now and report back when it's done and everything is secured."

"Yes, sir." Terrence disconnected.

That should take care of that, Bruegel thought to himself as he crawled back into bed.

No one, not even Kelior, knew the full scope of the plan. Victor could easily deny any knowledge and had no apparent motive for being involved.

No chance of discovery, Victor assured himself. However, sleep would not come when he tried to dismiss the concern. He sat up and lifted the receiver again.

When Terrence answered, Victor spoke. "You understand who must take the blame for these disposals?"

"That goes without saying, sir," Terrence answered in his usual monotone. "It will generate more business."

Chapter 6

"What did he say?" Dani hovered, unable to sit still as Ben put down the phone. In light of what he had discovered on the Persand Web site, he had decided to call Fontenot immediately, at his home number.

"He'll get us the video tomorrow, but he had already compiled a lot of info since I last spoke with him about the robbery. Apparently a client arrived almost immediately after the transfer was made and arranged for most of the money to go to an account in Geneva. The new account belongs to a corporation that was already set up with the Swiss bank. I have the name, but he couldn't give me the account number until tomorrow. I can't hack that without some serious consequences that even you couldn't iron out. I'm sure both will be useless by then anyway."

"Oh, goody," she muttered darkly. "This was a wasted trip."

"No it's not. We'll get the video and have a face that could provide an identity." He gave a bitter laugh. "I'm more interested than ever in seeing that face now."

"Why's that?" she asked, thumbing through her notes.

"Because this fellow managed to drop one of my business cards. While he was providing his own fake identity papers."

"How interesting," Dani said, her eyes narrowing on her notebook as she recorded it. "Pretty clumsy attempt, though."

"I *am* innocent," he told her, sounding too defensive, even to his own ears.

"I know," she said, still scribbling.

Ben copied what he had downloaded from the computer onto a slender flash drive and sat back, tapping the arms of his chair with his fingers.

"Crap. I couldn't back out fast enough," he grumbled. "Not even sure if it was possible, given our spotty connection here. The download took longer than I hoped. They're on to us at Persand."

Dani reached for her satellite phone. "Can they get a fix on our location?"

He shrugged. "Depends on their resources—yeah, probably—considering how fast they jumped on my tail. They followed me home, at least as far as the local island network."

She exhaled harshly. He watched as she punched in a speed dial number for Mercier. They had already spoken twice in the past half hour. "Jack, we're sending you what we've got for analysis." Her brow furrowed slightly. "Okay, done."

She clicked off and turned to Ben. "Send everything, even all the encrypted stuff, org charts—all of it. Attach it to an e-mail." She rattled off the government address. "Our transmission might be picked up, but they likely already know we've got the data."

Ben switched to his mail program and sent the information. They watched the screening bar as the green squares progressed. The files took nearly a minute to process. "This is so insecure it's not funny."

"Yeah, be interesting to see what they do about it, won't it?"

Ben thought *interesting* wouldn't quite cover it if what he suspected was true.

She had fallen into deep thought again. Her features looked pinched and her color had faded. He was about to try to snap her out of it when she blinked and stared at him.

"We should get out of Dodge," she declared, jumping up. "Right now."

She bit her bottom lip. "I'm sorry, Ben. You shouldn't be involved in this and the danger of it is a fact. We have to leave here right away. I'll keep you safe."

He laughed out loud, closed his computer and zipped it in its case. "Ah, Ms. Sweet, you are a real piece of work."

"No, I'm serious. We need to leave the Caymans immediately. Let's get our things together and get out of here." When he didn't move immediately, she added, "You *did* promise your mother you'd stay safe."

Ben didn't detect any sarcasm in the reminder, and what she said was true. "What about the video and the details Fontenot has for us? We can't leave now."

She pointed to the phone. "Call him. Tell him to send it to Mercier. Trust me, we need to get out of here *now*."

"Okay, if you really think the danger's that great. Meet you outside in the hall in five minutes. You have a plan?"

"Get to the airport as fast as possible and hope we can get a flight out." Her urgency was contagious.

"Maybe Fontenot can help us there. I'll call him now."

She looked at the clock on the bedside table. "Do it fast."

Ben shook his head as he put through the call to Fontenot.

She clutched his forearm for a second as she turned to go. "See you in a few."

Ben didn't move until the door connecting their rooms closed behind her.

She believed him. The thought produced a genuine grin. She even wanted to protect him. He didn't need that, but it felt good. He was back in the game, even if it was only temporary.

"Hey, Jim. Ben Michaels here," he said as Fontenot answered. "Need another favor." Even calling in favors brought back old times.

Dani hurriedly dressed in a lightweight coral pantsuit Carol had loaned her. Her navy shoes didn't match it. The jacket and pants were a bit loose. Sis must have put on a few pounds even before she got pregnant.

Her bag was stuffed with clothes, winter outfits she had brought with her for the visit, a few summer things borrowed from Carol's closet. No one knew how long this op would last or where it would take her. She adjusted her shoulder holster and buttoned up so it wouldn't show, then rolled her bag out into the hall.

She waited impatiently for Ben beside the elevator until he exited his room with his small weekender. A feeling of impending doom washed over her again. *Unsafe. Get away.*

"Jim offered his boat," he told her. "It's docked a

half mile away at the marina. We'll probably have to hoof it at this time of night."

"Not a problem," she assured him. The elevator opened and they got on. Dani willed the thing to hurry, wondering if they should have taken the stairs. Ridiculous thought. They were on the top floor and rolling suitcases.

The hotel smelled of doom and had since right after Ben hacked into Persand's records. Sometimes a premonition took that form, concentrating on only one of her senses. Peculiar scent this time, one she didn't recognize other than its definite link to danger. The desk clerk was dozing as they exited. The few people still in the bar were quiet, not even glancing their way. The streets looked deserted, giving the place an otherworldly feel.

Dani breathed deeply as they walked, exhaling that miasma of evil that had pervaded, enjoying the mixed outdoor scents of the local flora, booze and salt water. "I've never been here before," she said. "Have you?"

"Nope," he admitted. "Too bad we won't be here long enough to enjoy it."

His step was light, his gaze alert. The man was enjoying every minute of this little trip, no matter what he had promised his mama.

"So we head for Switzerland to see who shows up to claim the money," Dani said, quickening her step.

The feeling was coming back. The scent. And heat this time. Scorching heat. She began to sweat beneath her borrowed suit.

She tried to push the feeling aside. They were safe now, out of the hotel where she had sensed the danger was. Maybe this was just a leftover wave of warning to get well away. In a hurry. She walked even faster.

"Whoever gets the money or transfers it will have to provide identification just like the guy did here," Ben was saying. "Gone are the days when you could zap the stuff around anonymously. I just wish they hadn't picked *my* bank." He said it as though every red cent in that bank belonged to him, Dani thought.

He continued, "Fontenot said we could take his boat to Cayman Brac and fly out from there. He'll send someone over to pick it up."

"I'm glad our buddy Fontenot's being this accommodating," Dani said. "They're coming after you, after *us,* for hacking into their files," she told him honestly. "I feel it."

"You really think they will?" he asked, stopping for a second and glancing around them.

"I *know* it," she declared, unwilling to explain how she knew.

"Then hang on a minute," he said, taking out his cell phone.

Though she had listened to his end of the conversation, Ben spelled it out for her after he put his phone away. "Fontenot's making flight reservations for us using his credit card so we can't be traced by yours. We'll head for Geneva by way of Toronto."

Dani stared at him. "You took me at my word. About the risk."

He reached down for the handle of his bag. "Your word's good, isn't it? And you *are* running the op."

She picked up her pace as they again headed for the marina. "You've done something like this before, haven't you?"

He smiled. "Now what would a banker be doing skulking around like a spy? I'm just getting into the spirit of the game, that's all. Using common sense."

"Just what did you *do* in the army?" she demanded.

"Waded through a lot of sand," he said lightly. "Well, shall we go sailing or you want to stand around and wait for the Cayman connection to show up?"

Dani tried a laugh, but it sounded more like a cough. "Am I being a little overdramatic?"

"And paranoid, too. Paranoia is our friend. What if we were followed as we left Virginia?"

He could be right. They could have been followed here. Or whoever was on the Cayman leg of this operation could have received word they were on their way. All she knew was that it was not safe to remain here. Thank goodness Michaels was buying into that without insisting on proof.

She shook her head and kept walking. They were

way too exposed walking down a dimly lit, deserted street rolling their luggage. The feeling was growing, intensifying, the one she thought would be left at the hotel. It was much stronger now than it had been there, and encompassed more than her sense of smell.

Her nerves were zinging like crazy and they didn't calm in the least when she stepped on the boat. There would be trouble here, she thought to herself, but they had nowhere else to go.

"Is this thing seaworthy?" she asked.

He surveyed the length of it. "A Beneteau thirty-footer. Good boat. She's old, but looks sturdy and should get us where we're going." He leaned to the side of the cabin entrance, then held up a key. "Right where Fontenot said it would be."

They stowed their gear in the tiny cabin and changed their shoes so they wouldn't slip on the deck. As he donned a sweatshirt over his short-sleeved pullover, Dani spied the Beretta tucked into the waistband of his cords.

"Loaded for bear, I see," she commented. "Be sure the safety's on. Don't want to get butt-shot." She glanced around. "Do we have a life raft? Vests?"

"Roger that." He pointed out the items. "You ever sailed before?" he asked.

"Duh. I'm from Iowa! I hope *you*'ve done this before and don't expect me to cut jibs or anything!" She made a face.

He laughed out loud. "Not a problem," he said. "We have a motor."

He leaped back up on deck and offered her a hand. Dani took it reluctantly. Touching him did things to her insides. She didn't like how she waited for the opportunity, how she craved it happening. The warm clasp of his large fingers closing around hers felt too intimate. She'd been alone too long, that was all.

She tugged away as soon as she reached his side, unwilling to let these powerful sensations dull the others, the ones their lives might depend on. "Can we leave now?"

"In a minute. First I need to check the fuel and make sure the radio works. Charts were posted below, did you see?"

Dani hadn't noticed. "You're very observant."

He clicked his tongue. "And careful, too. I have no desire to wind up lost in the Cayman trough."

"You do know what you're doing here, don't you?" she asked.

"We're about to find out." He pointed to one of the ropes that secured the craft to the dock. "Untie that, would you?"

Her gaze raked up and down the marina as she helped him cast off. "Let's get the hell out of here."

When they were some distance out, Ben cut speed, ordered Dani to take the wheel and grabbed the binoculars she had brought up from the cabin. He studied the shoreline.

The motor buzzed faithfully as they made their way to Cayman Brac, the second largest island of the Cayman group and the only other one with an airport.

Dani hurried below without a word as soon as he took over again, probably to call in and report.

When she returned, she moved in close so he could hear her over the roar of the motor. "Boss says you're officially off the case now," she said, firming her lips and fixing her eyes straight ahead.

No way in hell was he stepping down. Dani might be fully competent to carry this off. Her team might find someone with qualifications that matched his when it came to accessing the necessary data. But Ben meant to see it through no matter what.

He didn't waste breath arguing with her. He had an ace up his sleeve. They both knew the destination of the money and the account numbers. But Ben had learned, during his little mining expedition into the Persand site, the name of the individual most likely heading up this debacle. He hadn't given Dani that information and he wouldn't. Not yet, anyway. First he had to figure out why this was happening.

For a fleeting moment, he thought of his mom and how she would suffer if she found out he was smack in the midst of something potentially worse than what he had faced before. He knew she would just have to cope somehow.

He looked back over his shoulder toward Grand Cayman, now a mere slit of a shadow on the horizon, haloed by a faint glow of lights.

His pulse leaped and he faced forward again, urging more speed out of the aging craft.

"I said you're out of it, Ben!" Dani repeated, almost shouting.

"I heard you," he shouted back. "But I can't quit right now."

"You have to," she declared firmly, her voice hoarse. "Orders!"

"Sorry, the timing's just not good for me," he shouted.

"What do you mean?"

He took one hand off the wheel and jerked a thumb over his shoulder. "Look behind us."

Chapter 7

"Should we run without lights?" Dani asked.

"With this moon, we're visible with or without…but, yeah we should be able to see *them* better with our own lights off."

"Can't this thing go any faster?" Dani cried, pounding the console with the heel of her hand. "God only knows what they're in!"

"If it's a speedboat, we're screwed," he said. She had to read his lips. Then louder, he demanded, "How're you fixed for ammo?"

"Fifteen rounds," she told him. "Another clip in my bag."

"Go get it!" he ordered, his words sharp with command.

She hustled to retrieve it from the cabin and checked her weapon. When she returned to the deck, he cut the lights and she watched their pursuer closing the distance between them. The smaller boat bounced along the surface like a skipping stone. "Two occupants!" she informed Ben.

He cursed, his staid banker image gone completely. "We can't outrun 'em. So…" With a completely calm face he cut the boat into as sharp a turn as possible, nearly flipping it as he reversed their direction. "They can still see us but might not be able to tell what I'm doing until it was too late."

"What the hell *are* you doing?" Dani screamed. It took all the strength she had to hold on and not get slung overboard.

"Damn things don't run in reverse…. Get ready!" he shouted. "Lock one arm around the mast and keep it between you and them. When we get close, start firing. I want them ducking bullets, not steering. Got it?"

"You're gonna ram them?"

"Damn straight!" He throttled forward at top speed. The other boat kept coming, obviously planning to fly alongside for a clear shot.

When they were within fifty yards, Ben yelled, "Open fire!"

She braced her right wrist and let them have it. Five rapid rounds. Their windscreen crackled and the two men disappeared. She squeezed the trigger for another volley.

"Hang on!" she heard Ben yell. He jammed the hull of their runabout just off-center. The much lighter, speeding boat glanced off and flipped.

Dani imagined screams rising above the sound of the impact and the sharp whine of engines. She put five rounds in the bottom of their fiberglass hull.

Without pause, Ben veered off to the right at full speed and cut another turn, this one much wider, putting them back on course and well away from the capsized vessel.

Dani grabbed the binoculars to scan the wreckage. "No heads in the water," she reported, but continued to keep watch until they were out of sight. Then she lowered the glasses and smiled at him. "How's the timing now? You ready to quit?"

Ben laughed, facing the spray that blew over the windscreen. He cut her a smiling look.

The rest of the trip to Cayman Brac went off without a hitch, save Dani getting locked below in the head when the door handle stuck. He tried not to laugh, but seeing her fuming over such a minor mishap after the way she'd performed during the pursuit struck Ben as downright hilarious. She was still pouting when they reached the airport.

"C'mon, getting locked in the head could have happened to *anybody*," he said, chucking her under the chin. "You'll drink off that story for years."

She moved out of reach and fumbled in her shoulder purse for her hairbrush. She groomed her wind-blown hair quickly and absently handed the brush to him. He ran it over his short cut just to make her happy. "Thanks. Do I pass inspection?"

"Yes. And you have to go home now," she told him, her voice matter-of-fact, yet laced with regret. "Switch your ticket for a flight to Miami or Atlanta."

"Much cheaper to fly through Toronto when you go to Switzerland," he replied easily. "Want some coffee?"

She sighed, her shoulders slumping as she rolled her eyes. Lovely eyes, they were, too. "You. Can. Not. Go."

"Watch me. Have card, will travel." He pointed to the coffee shop and took her arm, guiding her over. "Now it's the 'have gun will travel' part that I'm worried about. Think they'll confiscate it if it's packed with my shaving gear?"

As soon as they got their coffee and sat down, she took out her phone, punched one of the numbers and handed it to him. "Here. *You* talk to Mercier. He's my boss and he's telling me to unload you, tout de suite. You want me to lose my job?"

"Yeah. Then I'll put you to work at the bank. Obviously we could use an armed guard."

That got an unwilling laugh from her. He took the phone and waited for Mercier to answer. They had spoken before so Ben knew what to expect.

"Yes, Dani? What's up?"

"Agent Mercier, this is Ben Michaels. Dani tells me you're cutting me loose. May I ask why?"

The man at the other end hesitated. "Where's Danielle?"

"Right here drinking coffee." He held the phone over to her. "Say hey so your control won't think I killed you and dumped the body."

"Hey, boss. I'm not dead. He won't quit," she said, granting Ben a smile of challenge.

Ben took back the conversation. "I'm seeing this through, with her or without her," he warned.

"I can have you arrested for obstructing justice. Put your ass in jail," Mercier warned.

Ben sighed. "Well, you'd have to catch me first, sir, and I think I can stay at least one step ahead long enough to finish this. I have all the pertinent information you need to track down these funds and find who's amassing them. You need me and I'm *doing* this."

"Put Dani back on the phone."

Ben gave it to her with a little flourish and picked up his coffee, exhaling dramatically with pleasure at the taste of it. Better than Starbucks by a country mile.

He didn't even bother to eavesdrop as Dani and

her boss hashed out their problem of what to do with him. He knew what the outcome would be. Mercier would have his dossier pulled by now and see that he was qualified. The man had only been giving him a way out of danger that would save face if Ben wanted it. He didn't.

God help him, he had missed the action. He had missed making a difference. Granting a long-time customer an extra tenth of a point interest on a CD just didn't do it for him. He needed to get back in the game, if only this one final time. Then he'd settle down to banking.

His mother would forgive him if he came home in one piece, and if she didn't know what he was up to in the meanwhile. And if he saw he wasn't going to do that, Ben didn't intend to come home broken like before. He knew it was the waiting to see if he'd make it, the worrying that he couldn't handle the changes necessary, the three surgeries and their aftermath. That's what had laid her low and nearly killed her by degrees. She would have handled it far better if he had died instantly. He would never put her through all that again. This time it was all or nothing.

Dani closed her phone and put it away. She stared at him over the rim of her cup, then she set it down. "Looks like you win."

Ben wasn't the least bit surprised. "Okay, off to Canada. Want a souvenir of the islands?" He reached in his pocket and handed her the small seashell he had picked up off the ground at the marina while they'd waited for a taxi. "For luck," he said with a smile.

"Are you superstitious?" she asked as she fingered the tiny shell, feeling the rough fan of striations on one side and the smooth mother-of-pearl surface on the other. Like the two sides of Ben Michaels.

"Having a talisman never hurts," he told her.

"Well, I hope you've got your rabbit's foot handy. I think we're gonna need more than this little keepsake."

He stood, smiled down at her, took their bags and headed for the departure gate.

With a grin, she tucked the shell in her pocket. Like he said, it couldn't hurt.

Dani kept glancing over at the sleeping Ben to see if he had morphed yet again. He had been all but shape-shifting from the moment she first encountered him. House cat to tiger. Back and forth he went. Deferential to commanding. Conservative to take-charge. Who was he really and what would he be when he opened his eyes the next time?

She had a sneaky feeling that the polite, staid-banker image was the false one, but he did it so convincingly. Mama's boy? Maybe. What was the story there?

The top of his passport peeked out of his jacket pocket. She eased it the rest of the way out for a cursory examination. Middle name Roarke. He was thirty-six. Six feet two. He had lost at least twenty pounds since this was issued, she noted. She glanced at his photo and did a double take. It wasn't him!

She peered closer. Well, it *could* be him, she realized, but at first glance she'd had to wonder. He had definitely had a nose job. His cheekbones looked less prominent. And all those laugh lines were missing now, as well as the jaunty mustache and mole on his left cheek. She studied his sleeping face and looked back at his photo. The earlobes were different. So was his hairline. What was going on here? She needed to talk to control immediately.

Careful not to wake Ben, she retreated to the toilet at the back of the plane and called Mercier. He picked up right away.

They discussed the robbery and all that had occurred since. For the sake of brevity, they stuck strictly to the facts, not adding any conjecture at this point.

The authorities had identified the dead man at the bank, and she filed away the information about him that Mercier provided.

Ben would find this interesting, Dani thought. She would wake him after the phone call and get his take on it, but first she had a few more questions needing immediate answers.

"Tell me about Ben Michaels. If this gets uglier than it already has, I need to know just how qualified he is," she told Jack. "Also, you need to know his face doesn't match his passport. Not exactly anyway. Something not right here, Jack."

Mercier hesitated, then sighed. "I'll have to give you the abbreviated version. He was Delta Force."

"Was?" Dani interrupted. "Why didn't you tell me before? What's up?"

"He and his team were on an extended mission in Afghanistan. He was trying to save a family targeted by the Taliban. Only, the fifteen-year-old son had been recruited as an SB."

Suicide bomber. Dani winced.

Jack cleared his throat. "They were relocating them when the boy detonated. Michaels and the driver of the truck were the only ones in the vehicle who got out alive. Michaels was given a medical discharge because of his injuries, which I understand were extensive."

"Oh my God, how bad? What was involved?"

"Face, right arm and hip mostly. He's fit for this op now, that's what's important. Totally recovered."

Dani sighed with relief.

Jack continued, "After a number of surgeries, he settled with his folks and took the position at the bank. His father is president of Beresford. Michaels has the education for banking, and experience, too. He had worked there throughout his college years to help his family and also defray fees not covered by his scholarships. He was fortunate to have that as backup when he had to leave the army."

Dani felt a catch in her breath, just imagining what Ben must have endured. "Thank God he made it through," she said, exhaling sharply with relief. "That explains a lot."

"Danielle?" Jack said, catching her before she could ring off. "I sense some personal interest. *Not wise here.*"

She wanted to demand why not, but she knew better. That was tantamount to admitting she already was involved. Jack would not be cautioning her if he didn't have a good reason, something more than just falling for someone she worked with. Jack had done that very thing with Solange, the woman he married, and he had never been into giving orders he couldn't abide by himself.

"Don't worry, boss," she said, trying to sound amused. "He is *so* not my type."

She glanced at the ceiling, waiting for a lightning bolt to strike her for the lie. For insurance, she mentally listed Ben's major faults as she saw them. Apron strings made from anchor rope, for one thing. Control freak, for another. And, of course, he was too damned good looking....

Yeah, a handsome-as-sin hero who could take over and save the day as easily as he could make nice with his mother. Lots wrong there, girl. Big, scary faults. Fate would probably send her an egg-hatched troll who couldn't punch his way out of a paper sack the next time around.

"We're investigating at this end, all agencies on it. Get what info you can from the banks—faces, names, et cetera. Call if you need backup," Jack told her and rang off without a farewell.

That was his custom. No goodbye, no farewell, no take care. She guessed that was to reassure his people that he knew very well that they had sense enough to watch their backs.

"Okay," she said to herself as she put the phone away.

Dani went forward to take her seat beside Ben. He stirred when she sat and her arm brushed his. A chance touch, one that made her tingle, no matter how innocent.

She inhaled deeply, drawing in the scent of after-shave mixed with his own unique essence. Yep, the sense of smell was arousing, even when slightly blunted by the recycled air of the cabin. Or maybe she was just getting too much or not enough oxygen. At any rate, he filled that one sense to capacity. No premonition of danger accompanied it, either.

She slid his passport back in place. Fascinated and free to explore him unnoticed, Dani examined his long dark eyelashes, the way his hair had been carefully styled to control a natural wave. Her hungry gaze traced the fine, smooth pores of his face and the too perfect line of his nose. Far too good-looking to trust.

Yet she couldn't help noting again the long hairline scar in front of his ear. For the first time she saw a similar one running parallel and just beneath his eyebrow. Unless she looked really closely, both were pretty much invisible. Were those the result of injuries sustained in that bombing? Unable to help herself, Dani rested her hand on his arm, just a light touch.

How long had it been since someone had touched her the way he had earlier? Oh, she got a brief hug, a perfunctory smack on the cheek from her sister and her brother in law about twice a year—once when she arrived to visit, next when she left.

There was the quick pat on the shoulder she had gotten from her boss. Only the one and that proved highly impersonal and almost reluctantly granted. Of course, there were outright grabs on the mat during hand-to-hand with her fellow operatives. Not exactly touches of comfort, of caring, or of anything resembling camaraderie. Not in a scrap for dominance.

Dani flatly refused to resort to massage. Oh, she knew the touted benefits of it, but that kind of impersonal contact left her cold and even more tense than before. Paid-for touches, she could do without.

She could have frequented the singles bars and got all the touching she could stand, but it would have been the wrong kind and she knew it.

No, she wanted touching with a capital *T*. A sweet slide of fingers over the curve of her neck and shoulder, a palm cupped beneath her breast, a fingertip tracing her lips. Touching.

Ben provided that naturally, God bless him. He knew what she wanted, what she craved more than anything. And he was using it to get under her skin. Or maybe into her pants, she didn't know. Okay, she could make a pretty good guess.

It was too bad she hadn't already found some guy with a little romance in his soul to provide for her, before now, so she wouldn't be so damn needy for the contact. Six years was a long time.

She'd had Kevin back then. His touch wasn't all that great, neither was his lovemaking. But at least she had felt somewhat normal in their relationship. And then Kev got marriage-minded and his mother freaked. The blow to Dani's pride had proved worse than a breaking heart.

She knew what that was like, too. William Cos had broken hers when she discovered he was a double agent, when he had pulled a gun on her and Sean, when he intended to kill them to preserve his cover. She could still see the disbelief on his face when she'd shot him. Like he hadn't thought she could do it?

Then she was alone again, missing the trust along with the touching. She didn't trust herself now, either, with men.

Never would she admit to anyone that she felt the need to be held, stroked, comforted, cared about. Nor would she ever say why. Carol probably understood it, though they could never discuss it.

They had grown up at Lambs of God Children's Sanctuary in Landesford, Iowa. The orphanage where their parents had left them had proven a sterile place with no warmth. Not one of the sanctimonious caretakers there had the least inclination to cuddle with a Gypsy child. *Romany spawn.* The two of them were labeled "devil's get" from the outset. Even at the young ages of five and three they were tainted beyond redemption, as far as those people had been concerned.

The only human touching they got there came from a fist around their upper arms, holding them still for the smack of the flat side of a Ping-Pong paddle. Only rarely were they allowed to be together long enough to hug one another.

Carol had fared a little better, maybe. She had fairer hair, normal brown eyes and lighter skin. Maybe those "favored" characteristics allowed her to develop a sweeter nature.

Dani had grown up belligerent, cocky and aggressive, all attributes that aided her in her occupation. She didn't regret them.

But her softer side had gotten buried deep. It wouldn't do to let it loose now, not on this op and not with Ben Michaels. What if she lost the benefits her hard shell gave her?

God, it was so hard not to respond to him. She could hardly help herself. But she knew in her heart there were differences too great for them to ever overcome if they became too close.

He was no fly-by-night lover. That just wasn't his style. He had family man written all over him. And she could never be one to settle down the way Carol had done, no matter how much she envied her sister.

Carol hadn't even told her husband about their background. She had confessed that she was raised in an orphanage, but not the animosity she had endured or the type of people who had put her there. Not many men would welcome a woman born of a grifter and his common-law wife, parents who couldn't be bothered with kids while they ran their scams across the country and lived out of rusty vans and ragged tents. She barely remembered any of it. Much of her background and abandonment, Dani had imagined, of course, but she had read as much as she could find about the Gypsies and their roving lifestyle.

She didn't need a preternatural premonition to tell her how Ben and his family would react if they discovered her past. Best not to put herself in a position of having to reveal it.

Chapter 8

Ben's eyes opened and he frowned, still half asleep.

Maybe what woke him was that little jolt of electricity that sparked whenever they touched. He felt it, too, she knew.

Dani smiled. He tried to stretch, then gave it up when there wasn't room.

"We there yet?" His voice was rough, gravelly.

"Not yet, but I have some good news for you."

"Ah, the plane's diverted to Tahiti, where we have a weeklong layover?"

"Even better. I called in and we now have a name for the dead perp. Ahmed Fayal, originally from

Saudi Arabia. Wealthy family. Educated at Syracuse University, business degree. Five years as a U.S. citizen. No priors, not even a parking ticket."

Ben grew fully alert instantly. "That was quick. I thought it would take a lot longer since he had no wallet or papers on him. And since his fingers…"

Dani sat up straight and glared at him. "How did you know about his fingertips?" She hadn't known. Just now Mercier had told her over the phone that the pads of the robber's fingers had been smooth as glass, the whorls that made identifying prints completely absent.

Ben's gaze remained steady. "Chief Talbert mentioned it when he was interviewing me, right after he checked out the body."

"Strange, he would offer *you* that information. He never said a word to me about it." For that matter, neither had Ben.

"So how did they discover who he was?"

"Fayal's wife went to the police about a month ago and reported that he had disappeared. One of those 'went out for a loaf of bread and never came back' deals. She filed a police report, scared he was dead, angry he might have run out."

"Our thief matched the description of the missing husband. However, when our people tried to make contact with the wife, they found her missing, as well. Still, our boy's toe prints matched some found on the tiles in the Fayal bathroom."

Ben rubbed his chin with his fingertips, a mannerism he had used before that seemed to accompany deep thought. "Who was *she?*"

Dani inclined her head and gave him a sly look. "You're really asking what nationality, right?"

He made a face. "Don't say that as if I'm a racist. I just want to know what we're dealing with here."

"She's from Rhode Island, a Caucasian born and raised there. Parents were high school teachers, English and history. She and her husband met in college about ten years ago and married right after their graduation. No children. No pets. Decent portfolio and little debt. Oh, and before you ask, she worked for Persand Inc., in marketing. Fayal did, too. He was an accountant."

Ben's eyes lit with excitement. "Persand?"

Dani nodded. "So what are you thinking?" she asked.

He traced the line of his chin again and his smooth brow furrowed a little. "That everyone investigating is meant to believe Fayal was a sleeper that activated. Called up markers for multiple contributions from those who would support the jihad. Then he compiled it all, taking a hefty sum from Persand to round it out. Of course, he had his cohorts on the Cayman end ready to spirit it away."

She frowned. "You don't think that's the case now, do you?"

"Maybe Fayal thought so, but I believe somebody was running the show, running *him* and for another reason. Somebody who knows me."

"But the money, Ben. You still think it's going to some terrorist organization?"

"Maybe, maybe not. For safety's sake, we have to assume it is. But it bothers me that they're leaving such a clear trail. Unless…" He frowned now, the fingers on his chin halting, tapping a few times. "You can make it disappear if you convert it to something else. A private, prearranged cash purchase of something more portable that would leave no trail."

"Such as?"

He shrugged. "Stones, probably. My guess would be diamonds. If they get those safely away, they could easily turn them back into cash in Saudi, Qatar, Jordan or wherever they plan to set up for business." His thoughtful look turned to a frown of resignation. "They didn't want your people to get your hands on the funds, or to freeze them before they could convert them. But they wanted them floating around just long enough for my name to come up several times in connection with the deal."

"But why?"

"Don't know, but I'll find out."

She sighed. "I hope you know something about the diamond trade, because I know *zilch*."

"I know a little," he admitted.

"Do you think they'll convert it in Switzerland?"

"Assuming they go for diamonds, I'd say Amsterdam, but that's probably too obvious. The thing is, I expect they were counting on having a little time between the actual money transfer and the discovery of the missing funds by the auditors. Now they're aware we're on to them and are trying to get rid of us."

"And if they had each step lined up to happen almost instantly, our being on the trail wouldn't present any problem, would it?"

"Right," Ben said. "They might even stand back and enjoy watching us dashing around, scratching our heads and wondering how the devil they got away with it." He stroked his chin again, then tapped it thoughtfully. "It makes me wonder if they've realized who you are yet."

"What do you mean?" she asked.

He shrugged, fanning his fingers. "Well, it makes no sense that they'd try to kill you if they know the feds are onto them already. What purpose would that serve? There are an endless supply of agents who would replace you and killing an agent would really set the dogs on them." He shook his head. "You weren't on the newscasts. Never mentioned you at all except as the one bank customer present. Didn't even give your name."

"I had a word with the chief about that. Low profile and all that. So who do they think we are?"

"A pissed-off banker who suspects what's up and is out to prove it. You? I don't know. My guess would be, they simply want to get rid of us as loose ends and prevent anyone going higher up with the investigation."

"I wonder if they'll have people there waiting for us when we get to Switzerland."

He settled back and closed his eyes again, his arms folded across the wide breadth of his chest. "Maybe. Unless they plan to strike before then."

Wonderful.

In Toronto, the plane landed a bit early and Dani rushed to the ticket counter and traded up for a different connecting flight. Instead of a six-hour wait, she managed to secure seats on one that was already boarding, destination Geneva.

All the while, she had been reviewing what had happened thus far. As soon as they were seated, she turned to Ben. "Fayal obviously had a partner watching your bank."

Ben nodded. "A partner who either followed us or called a contact on Grand Cayman to relate when we'd be arriving."

"You think they might go after Fontenot?"

He wore a worried expression. "Yes, I do. Could you get someone from your outfit to see if they can locate him?"

"Mercier's on it already. We'll know before we land." She glanced around surreptitiously. "You don't think we could have been followed, do you?"

Ben sat back, unfastened his seat belt and settled in for the flight. "Whoever was after us on Grand Cayman, assuming there were more than two who chased us, who are probably dead, won't know we flew out of Cayman Brac until they discover the runabout capsized."

"*Probably* being the keyword. What if one of the gunmen had a way to contact help after they went down?"

He frowned and sat up a little straighter.

Neither of them wanted to pursue the possibility of survivors at the moment.

He leaned back and closed his eyes. Sleep, the great escape, Dani thought with a sigh. No way would she get a wink on this flight.

She had suffered too many of her little Gypsy spells since that belated one at the bank. Worse, they had begun blending together in undulating waves of warnings. No definition. Totally useless. Maybe she ought to report that to Mercier.

Ben's hand found hers and enclosed it, his thumb gently stroking the tips of her fingers. His eyes were still closed, his smooth forehead uncreased by lines of concern, his expression composed as if he hadn't a worry in the world.

* * *

"Where did you get that? Give it here!" a high-pitched voice demanded. "That is not yours, Carter! Hand it over."

Startled out of a fretful nap, Dani leaned over in the aisle and looked toward the front of the plane. Oh, she was feeling something now, big-time. Alarms were ringing in her head like Chinese gongs gone crazy.

"Is, too! Finder's keepers! It was in my pack!" a childish voice complained. "Give it back!"

A couple of seats ahead and across the aisle, she saw a woman yank something away from her seat-mate and start to examine it. It appeared to be a small laptop computer or maybe a DVD player.

Dani's heart leaped to her throat, all warnings about things smuggled into passengers' bags flew through her head at the speed of light. *Danger! Danger! Danger!*

She jumped up, dashed forward and snatched the object from the woman and headed directly for the back of the plane. "Marshal." She addressed a suited gentleman who was sitting in the last seat alone. "We may have a situation here."

The woman from whom she'd grabbed the object was right behind her, complaining loudly. Dani had no time for this. She turned and snapped, "Be quiet and go sit down or I'll arrest you."

The woman backed away, her hand to her mouth.

"Carter didn't take that. Someone mistakenly put it in his carry-on. Please, he's not a thief! My son is—"

"Return to your seat, keep quiet and don't make me tell you again!" Dani ordered firmly. When she turned to speak to the marshal, she saw he wore a look of suspicion. His hand had disappeared beneath his jacket.

She hurriedly introduced herself. "I'm Agent Danielle Sweet with the COMPASS agency, HSA." She pulled out her badge, displayed it and tucked it away. "I happened to overhear that mother's discovery of this." She held out the mini laptop. "Might be exactly as she said and someone stuck it in the wrong bag."

"Or it might not," the marshal said, handling it gingerly. "Joseph LeFleur, Air Marshal. How did you recognize me?"

"Got that look about you," Dani said with a shrug. Plus, she'd noticed the bulge of a holstered weapon in his coat when she used the toilets earlier. "So what do you think? Ditch it in the drink to be on the safe side, right?" *Get it off this plane! Now!* Her mind was screaming. She could barely manage her panic, but knew she'd better not come off as hysterical or it might delay things to the point of disaster.

"Could I see it?" a deep voice said just behind her. *Ben.*

"Who are *you?*" the marshal demanded, squinting up at Ben, one hand inside his jacket again.

"My partner, Ben Michaels," Dani explained, fudging a little. "We have to get this off the plane, Ben," she said.

"I have EOD training," Ben explained. "Can I help?"

Dani stepped back as the marshal stood. She was nearly jumping up and down. "I say we eject it. We're over open water," she said, trying really hard to sound calm. "Better safe than sorry."

Ben looked at her, his gray gaze piercing. She noted new little crow's feet formed at the outer corners of his eyes. No wonder, she thought. Her own hair had probably grayed in the last five minutes. "Surely you don't think—"

"This might have absolutely nothing to do with us or the bank situation," she reminded him urgently.

"I agree we should ditch it," he said to LeFleur. His speech was more clipped than his usual drawl. "If this is rigged, it's probably triggered by opening the lid. Or maybe by cabin pressure at a certain altitude. It looks perfectly normal, but there's no way to tell without the right equipment to test it. I think Dani's right," he said to the marshal. "Let's get it off the plane."

He looked over at her. "Go forward, explain things to the crew while we jettison the thing." He turned to the marshal. "You know where to go to do that?"

"Hatch in the cargo hold," the marshal said.

"Dani?" Ben said, reaching for her hand. He gave

it a comforting squeeze. Both knew there was nothing to say, but the look in his eyes spoke volumes. She spoke back with hers. *Wish we'd had more time. Wish we'd met under other circumstances. Wish we'd made better use of the time we had.*

"Let's go!" the marshal prompted. He seemed to want it over with in a hurry now that the decision had been made.

Dani left them without a backward look and hurried forward. The passengers weren't clueless, weren't calm, either. Word had spread like a brush-fire: Bomb onboard.

"Everyone sit down and buckle up," she shouted, more to give them something seemingly positive to do than to insure their safety. If that thing exploded, they were all toast. "Stay calm. Everything's under control!" She hoped.

She scanned faces as she went forward, but she knew the one who had planted that device was not onboard.

The flight attendants huddled between first and tourist, watching her. They looked as frightened as the passengers. Suddenly she realized they were scared of her! Small wonder, the way she had come barreling up the aisle shouting orders.

Dani quickly flashed her badge. "Homeland Security," she assured them. "Please advise the cockpit crew that we have a potential explosive onboard. The marshal and my partner are disposing of it."

She grasped the arm of the nearest attendant and gave her a little shake. "Go to the cockpit and let your captain know they're about to jettison the object— *now!*" Dani shoved her none too gently, then turned to the other attendants.

"Wipe the fear off your faces and calm those passengers. They're edging toward panic." She grasped the arm of the closest attendant. "Keep an eye out for anyone suspicious. You know the drill."

They hopped to it. Dani breathed a sigh of relief and started for the front of the plane.

A thunderous explosion rocked Dani off her feet and the aircraft made a sudden lurch. She hit the floor with a thud. *Oh God, this was it!*

Chapter 9

Screams deafened her to anything else. Dani scrambled upright expecting any second to be blown to smithereens. Not the way she had wanted to go. Better than burning alive, she reckoned. Adrenaline poured through her veins like jet fuel.

After several seconds passed, she found she was through the first-class section and at the door of the cockpit. She pounded on it, knowing they wouldn't let her in. Why would they? She could be a terrorist trying to take over.

To her surprise, it did open. The huge man who held it had a weapon pointed directly at her nose.

Then she saw his uniform and realized he was one of the crew.

"Don't shoot! Agent Dani Sweet!" She gasped, thrusting her badge at his face.

He moved his head back to focus. "Joe Conger, copilot," he muttered. "You're not the marshal." He frowned at her credentials as he read them.

"No," she admitted. "LeFleur is. He and my partner were disposing of the bomb."

"You're a passenger?" He glanced past her for possible threats, then lowered the .45, one Dani knew shot slugs designed not to penetrate the aircraft and cause a loss of cabin pressure.

And speaking of pressure, that seemed stable at the moment. Things weren't flying around. Turbulence caused her to sway, but the plane itself seemed to be flying okay, and not on a downward spiral. Passengers who could scream could also breathe, and a number of them were screaming hard.

"My partner and I are on a case," she told him. "Nothing to do with this." Or so she hoped.

"Any activity in the back?" Conger asked, again peering past her down the aisle.

She knew what he meant. Had anyone stood and made demands, given any indication they were responsible for the bomb, taken any hostages?

"Someone slipped the thing into a kid's carry-on before he boarded. How bad was the damage, can you tell yet? Can you bring us down safely?" Dani asked.

He sighed, shaking his head. "Detonation was right outside the plane. Close. Portions of the landing gear were damaged, and pressure in the hold is screwed."

He wiped his brow with his forearm and backed inside the cockpit. "There's either a hatch still open or part of the bay's floor is missing."

Dani's heart skipped. Ben was down there, injured, unable to breathe—or gone through that hole in the cargo bay and down to the North Atlantic.

She couldn't let herself think of that. They had a plane full of passengers to get on the ground.

"Can we turn around and make land?" Dani asked, trying to focus on the passengers, the condition of the plane, anything but her terror over Ben's fate.

"Closer to make for Iceland," the copilot told her. "We've already radioed for clearance."

All right, there was nothing else she could do here. "I need to see about the marshal and my partner." Dani stopped for a second to catch her breath and get her imagination in hand. "They went down to cargo to get rid of the bomb. At least they got it outside the plane before it blew. If the pressure's dropped down there—"

"Let's go," the copilot said abruptly. "Come on. There's no telling what the blast did." He swallowed hard. "Or if they even survived it."

Dani prayed all the way. They entered a small elevator that lowered them to the belly of the aircraft. The air there was arctic. And thin. The noise was deafening.

Nearby, LeFleur lay on his back with a massive head wound. Dani began to pray again before she heard a voice.

"Help me cover the hole!" Ben shouted, struggling with an enormous storage container.

Dani and the copilot added their weight to the metal container and managed to slide it over a gaping three foot aperture that looked straight down into the clouds.

The copilot motioned toward the elevator. Individually they ascended. Gathering in the service area, they leaned against the walls to catch their breath.

"Will that weight over the hole work?" Ben gasped.

"Hope so," the copilot said. "What happened to the marshal?"

Ben clenched his eyes shut and grimaced. "He dropped the device out and was closing the small hatch when the bomb blew, shredding the edges of the aluminum. The metal door caught him in the head as it blew off the hinges. Everything went to hell then. I could see sky. Thought that hole might continue to rip if I didn't get it closed up."

"I'm just glad we found you alive!" Dani told him, feeling tears nearly choke off her words. She never cried, but she sure felt like it now.

Ben said nothing and refused to lean on her as the copilot ushered them into the half-full section of first class. "I'll go see if we can get the old girl on the ground. Chances are we can slide her in if we have to. These 767's are sturdy as hell, but a couple of prayers wouldn't hurt." With that, he rushed back to the cockpit door and disappeared inside.

Dani placed a hand on Ben's arm and felt him jerk away from her. She continued to observe him anyway, trying to check his pupils without being too obvious, wondering if he was concussed.

He didn't want her to touch him for some reason. He rubbed his chin in that same gesture he used often, as if he were feeling for something beneath the skin. Only now he pressed harder, so hard his fingertips turned white.

"Are you all right, Ben?" she asked.

He immediately dropped his hand to the armrest, gripped it and nodded. "Yeah, I'm fine." His eyes met hers. "You?"

Dani smiled wryly and cocked her head. "I'm still in one piece. Wouldn't have given *you* odds on that a little while ago. It was a damn close call."

She traced his sleeve lightly. "Ben, I know it was hard, watching LeFleur buy it. He was a brave agent, doing his job. If I had to go, that's how I'd want it."

He laughed bitterly. "Tell his family that. I'm sure they'll appreciate the sacrifice."

She clutched his forearm and shook it. "Think of the lives you and he saved today. There are at least a couple of hundred people on this plane. All alive because of the two of you."

He frowned at her and the muscle beneath her fingers flexed like bowing steel. "And he might be dead because you and I took this plane, ever thought of that?"

Dani nodded. "Yeah, I did think about it."

"Someone called ahead. Child's play to follow us to the gate, get in line, stick the bomb in a carry-on that's boarding."

Dani thought about that. "How did they get it through the security checkpoint? It should have been X-rayed."

Ben nodded. "Oh yes, and we *all* know exactly what a little DVD player is supposed to look like inside, don't we? Especially those of us who are hired for minimum wage with a couple of weeks training. Even with all your security classes, do *you* know? Unless there are little cartoon dynamite sticks with fuses, how would you know if it was rigged?"

She blew out a breath of frustration. "Point taken. So you think these people who are after us have a network large enough to cover all the major cities we might fly from?"

He sighed and closed his eyes and rubbed his forehead. "I don't know. I just don't know."

Dani reached inside her shoulder purse and retrieved her cell phone. "Time to call in backup. Mercier needs to give me a list of our assets in Switzerland and Amsterdam, in case we wind up there. We'll need ammo and safe houses, maybe even a couple more operatives. Assuming we get off this crippled plane alive in Iceland, we're going to need a good sized network of our own."

"Iceland?" Ben asked, then chuckled. "Well, if there's any trouble when we reach *there,* I think we have to assume this is a whole lot bigger than even *I* imagined."

Dani laughed a little. "They can't know where we're landing, which is good. We need a short breather. At least, I do."

"What we need is a way into Europe that won't leave a trail a mile wide," he said. "Any ideas?"

"Sextant can provide us with a private plane, but it will take about five or six hours to get it authorized and flown to Keflavik."

Ben smiled. "There's your breathing room, but I expect we'll be inundated with questions once we're safely down. Can you pull a few strings and get us off with a brief report?"

She handed him the small notebook from her pocket and a pen. "Start writing while I make the call. Let's have our reports ready." At least it would give them something to do besides worrying about the plane's landing.

Twenty minutes later, the pilot came on the intercom to advise everyone to take the precautions necessary for a crash landing. The atmosphere within Tourist had already escalated to barely controlled hysteria. First Class passengers were quieter, probably inebriated, she reckoned, on the house.

Ben took her hand in his. He didn't bother with a lie of reassurance.

"Are you afraid?" she asked him.

"Sure, but we've done all we can do. That's some consolation, right?"

"Yeah," she answered, giving his hand a squeeze. "All we could do."

Dani tried to concentrate on something other than the impending descent. She focused on the warmth and comfort of Ben's hand, the way it encompassed her smaller one, how his thumb caressed the back of her knuckles.

The gesture seemed very intimate, as if they had once been lovers and still needed this warm connection. Maybe in a former life—no, she didn't really believe in reincarnation. Still, there was something so familiar, so right, about the feel of his hand clasping hers.

They might very well crash and burn. Much would depend on the ground crews and whether the runway was properly prepared. Out of their control. All they could do was hope and pray conditions were right. And hold hands.

"Would you kiss me, Ben?" she asked, aghast the second the words left her mouth.

He smiled sweetly and looked directly into her eyes. "My pleasure." His mouth lowered to hers, his lips gentle. His free hand cupped the side of her face, his thumb grazing her cheek. Dani opened her lips and he deepened the kiss.

Turbulence rocked the plane, causing their teeth to graze, but he didn't break the kiss. Dani buried her mind in the warmth of his mouth, the caress of his tongue and the feel of his hands against her skin.

His groan reverberated inside her. She wished they were locked together in an embrace, but everything prevented that. Slowly he released her mouth. "Time to get ready," he said, handing her the pillow he had been leaning on as he slept. "Put this on your knees and lean forward." He did the same, facing her, his gaze holding hers.

She still saw no fear in his eyes. Maybe he had come to terms with death. "I'm glad I'm with you," she told him.

He grinned. "I just wish we were together somewhere else right now."

"Me, too." Her voice broke off with a sharp cry when the plane bounced off the ground. They listed rapidly to one side and a wing caught the ground. A huge ripping sound sent them spinning horizontally. And then they flipped.

Chapter 10

When Dani came to, she was hanging sideways in her seat. Screams assaulted her ears. Ben fought to release his seat belt then began working on hers. They fell onto the people across the aisle who were still strapped in.

Most of the passengers were in shock, but Dani noted no apparent fatal injuries in those she could see. It took sharp orders and a few harsh shakes to get some of them moving. The stronger ones recovered, panicked and began trampling the others to get out.

Ben's military training surfaced immediately and he started issuing commands, establishing what order he could.

"Release your seat belts and go that way!" he shouted above the din of panic surrounding them. "Be calm!" He was moving from seat to seat, repeating his orders, bracing his feet on the legs of the seats to stay upright in the slanted aisle.

Dani offered reassurance where she could, shamed several others into helping and generally did all she could to evacuate the plane, following Ben's lead. The attendants were working from the front, doing the same, unhooking passengers and ushering them toward the open door.

Getting to it necessitated a steep climb up a skewed aisle, a disorienting trip punctuated by passengers' fearful cries and the screams of sirens outside.

Ben had worked his way to the forward door. He and one of the male attendants were shoving individuals out the door, down an inflated chute to the runway.

Dani tried to see out the windows, but where one side showed only the littered surface of the runway, the other displayed only sky.

Ben grabbed her arms as she neared the door. "Get away from the plane quick as you can!" he warned. "Hit the ground running!"

"I'm not going without you!" she cried, but felt him lift her off her feet and toss her down the chute just as he had the others.

Dani got her feet under her after her rapid descent and stationed herself at the bottom of the inflated ramp. Passenger after passenger, she helped get people running for safety as smoke poured from the fuselage.

A terrible scent began filling her nostrils. Flames licked at the wing rising above them like an angry finger pointing to the sky. The other had broken off and lay torn, twisted and upside down well away from the main wreckage.

At last, Ben appeared beside her, grasped her arm and hauled her along beside him until they reached the crowd of rescued passengers. Crews from a half dozen ambulances tended to the injured while fire trucks hose down the wreckage with foam.

"They've got it under control, I think," Ben said. "Everybody's out." He turned to her, running his hands over her shoulders and arms. "Are you hurt?"

"No," Dani answered, reveling in his touch. She badly needed to be touched. "Were you?"

"Since we don't need aid, let's find whoever's in charge and get this over with."

She went to break off, but he didn't move. Instead he looked down at her. "But first…"

And as Dani's head swirled with feeling he pulled her close and kissed her as if his very life depended on it.

She threw her arms around his neck and took the life-affirming kiss for what it was. Adrenaline-induced euphoria. Make that *ecstasy*. God, the man could kiss!

When he drew away, he laughed, lifted her up and whirled her gently around as if she weighed nothing.

Dani braced her hands on his shoulders and looked down into his eyes. Beautiful eyes full of relief and happiness. The sexual tug on her senses was overpowering. He felt it, too. Didn't even try to hide it. His gray eyes softened and his lips quivered.

For a long moment, they simply admitted silently what they were feeling. They were unashamed and enjoyed it, even though she knew it could only be temporary.

Later, in the hotel room they'd taken to rest in, as he and Dani waited for her team's plane to Europe, Ben wished he had kept his mouth shut about his suspicions regarding the bank robbery. Maybe if he hadn't gotten Dani involved, he could have spared her the risk. And he was still feeling guilty over LeFleur's death.

"You're taking this too personally," Dani told him, as if reading his mind. "You can't do that."

She sat resting against the pillows of the queen-size bed. They had rooms at the Northern Lights hotel near the airport. Ben sat across her room in the chair, too antsy to relax; he had come to her room to discuss their plans once they arrived in Switzerland.

"You have to distance yourself, Ben. It's the only way."

"I know," he said, pretending to agree with her.

Unfortunately he was not able to do that. He had lost his objectivity a long time ago when he had witnessed lives snuffed out in an instant of unnecessary madness.

Now, at least for him, every act of violence was personal. Terrorism was personal. To hell with all that claptrap about holy wars and restructuring society. If someone wanted to kill you, for whatever reason, that was pretty damn personal in his book.

These people, these financiers who were clients of his own bank, were obviously all for the killing. They lived off the bounty available to them through their American-based businesses. Maybe using U.S. dollars to finance the destruction of the Western world appealed to their sense of irony, to their screwed-up tastes.

At any rate, he felt personally responsible for doing all he could to prevent that money from reaching the wrong hands.

Dani tossed a stray pillow at him. "Hey, we're supposed to be winding down."

Noticing her, Ben shook off the doom and gloom. Here he was with a beautiful woman, a courageous one who was using all her resources to accomplish the same ends as him. There was nothing either of them could do until they reached their destination, and the plane to take them there wasn't due for another three hours. He *should* unwind.

He got up and held out his hand to her. "Come on."

"Where are we going?" she asked, a tentative smile playing around her lips.

"Blue Lagoon. You want to relax, that's the place."

He stopped at one of the airport shops and purchased swimsuits with his credit card. A short cab ride later and they were there.

The enormous Lagoon was an otherworldly place, man-made, but you'd never guess it if you didn't know. The wide expanse of geothermically heated water was a soothing blue and crystal-clear. The sulfuric smell became less noticeable after you'd been in a while. The heavenly feel of it made that negligible.

"Man, I could get used to this," Dani said, floating on her back, sighing with contentment.

Ben found peace in just watching her, enjoyed the sight of her face and breasts just visible above the surface. She abandoned herself so naturally and completely to the pleasure, he wanted to do the same.

He lay back and closed his eyes, his fingers linked loosely with hers so they wouldn't drift apart. The air was cold, bracing to breathe in. The waters were warm, well above body temperature. Steam rose off the wavelets, creating a haze that blocked out the sight of other bathers.

He couldn't remember when he had ever felt this good, this alive. "Living in the moment," he muttered. "Wish we could always do that."

"I try," she admitted as she stood, the water lapping at her chin. She smoothed back her hair with her free hand. "I think after all that's happened, I might try a little harder."

Ben knew exactly what she meant. Difficult to take life for granted after almost losing it. And she had almost lost hers three times in the past twenty-four hours. The very thought of that gave him chills.

Unable to stop himself, Ben reached for her and enfolded her in his arms, wishing he could protect her from everything. He just needed to do that, more than he needed to breathe.

She allowed him to hold her for a while, then pushed away, smiling, when his hands slid over her slender curves and came to rest against her back just below her waist.

"Not exactly what I meant by living in the moment..." she said, looking a little nervous. He realized his groin had been pressing against her.

She raked her hair back again and looked toward the hotel. "We should go back and get dressed."

Ben didn't mind. He couldn't make love to her out here. He shouldn't at all, anywhere. But their coming together seemed fated to happen sooner or later. Later would probably be best, maybe just before they went their separate ways. Sooner, and he might get too used to it. Hell, he might get addicted. And he might not be able to let her go when the time came.

With a sigh of resignation, he led her out of the ethereal blue waters of the lagoon and back into the real world.

They found a taxi and soon reached the hotel, where he walked her to her room. "Here you are, back safe and sound," he said, pushing her wet hair back behind her ears. "We have a little time before we have to go."

She nodded, reaching up to run her hand down the side of his face. "A little time." Those amber eyes offered him a stunning invitation.

No sooner had the door closed than he had his arms around her and was pressing her against the wall. "I want you," he gasped between kisses so hot he felt flames.

She writhed so sensuously, fitting herself to him, answering him with her own need. No hesitation. No coy withdrawals. No denial. This was it, Ben thought. This was the instant he had survived for, his reason for being here. His reason for being, period.

He swept her over to the bed and crashed them down onto it. Ben abandoned himself to instinct, to her cues, to the needs that drove them. Dani did not want gentle, not the way she grasped and demanded.

Clothing flew this way and that as they clawed it away. He was desperate to feel her skin next to his. Her breasts were high and firm, dark nipples beaded in invitation. He laved and nipped, loving the sounds she made, wordless demands. Not one to beg, his Danielle. She took. But she gave, as well. And then gave more. Ben slid his palms down her sides, around her firmly muscled thighs and raised her legs, cradling himself between them.

"Now!" she said, attempting to guide him into her by moving her hips. "Ben?"

"Not yet. Protection." He didn't have any. Damn.

"I'm okay, on the pill. Now!"

Still Ben held back. "You trust me, right? That I'm okay? I am."

"Me, too," she muttered, her frantic nodding all the encouragement he needed. "I'm good."

He entered her by degrees, fearing if he took her all at once, it would be over before he got started, and surely before she was ready. This needed to last.

He tried counting backward, tried thinking base-ball scores, tried breathing exercises. But the sheer heat of her body closing around him, the sweet slide of sex, the pure scent of her, blocked his mind to everything else in the world.

She set the pace and he increased it, as unable to control the impulse as he had been unable to guide that rocketing plane to the ground. All he could do was abandon himself to flight and hope for the best.

Her fingers plowed through his hair. Her mouth grasped his, claiming it as he claimed hers. Her hips rose to meet his thrusts, a throw right over the edge of reason. "Come with me," he pleaded, hating her for ending it, loving her for ending it, wanting it again even before he finished with a soul-deep groan of fury.

She shuddered violently, clasping him so tight he thought she'd burrow into him and never let him go. Then her hands softened on his shoulders and slid down like silk along his arms. "Oh, my," she whispered.

Heaven had nothing on her. He felt empty and filled at the same time. Humbled and prideful. Saved and destroyed.

He knew in that moment, lying with her in his arms, that he would never be the same again. He didn't even contemplate whether that was a good or a bad thing. It simply was.

Yeah. Ben closed his eyes, feeling little aftershocks ripple through him directly from her.

Chapter 11

Dani would have kicked her own behind if she could have reached it with her foot. At least she had been able to get him out, not that he had gone willingly. Damn, she'd had to invent an excuse to make him leave so to not hurt his feelings.

It wasn't his fault she was such an idiot.

The shower hadn't restored her sanity, either, and her attempt at a nap had been a joke. How could she sleep in that bed where he had...they had...?

Not wise to relive *that* or she'd be calling him back over. She threw off her robe, yanked on her clothes and cursed when her pants zipper stuck momentarily. Damn it all, she had to keep her wits about her. Next thing she knew, she'd be losing her heart to the man. *Then* what?

Yeah, he was the kind of man to steal it, she warned herself yet again. Maybe if she could have continued to think of him as a banker with a doting mama who would hate her guts, Dani could have written him off for good. But he was much, much more than that. He had served his country, been severely wounded doing so and had managed to rebuild his life afterward. She had seen his bravery in the face of death. He was a man who would leap between her and a bullet. On purpose. That was definitely hard to resist…even though she didn't need his protection, she reminded herself.

But he had the most wonderful hands. And mouth. And…

Dani sucked in a deep breath and huffed it out. She could look after herself, but just the fact that he wanted to protect and defend her touched her somewhere deep, at a dangerous level.

She had sorely longed for that feeling of security while growing up—that was it. Any psychologist would tell you straight-out that was the reason she felt this way. Ben surely wouldn't appreciate being latched on to as a father substitute.

The thought of that dredged up a bitter laugh. She hadn't felt anything like daughterly with Ben. Ever.

Maybe it wasn't an Electra complex after all. Maybe she just wanted him like crazy.

She was securing her hair back in a sleek little knot at her nape when a knock on the door interrupted her thoughts. "Yes, who is it?"

"Me," Ben said.

Dani took another deep breath. Okay, she could do this. She could be casual. It wasn't as if she could avoid a face-to-face for long anyway. She straightened her jacket and opened the door, fully dressed now except for her bare feet. She forced a smile that felt wooden.

He came inside, obviously avoiding her eyes. Maybe she wasn't the only one who considered their roll in the hay a mistake. He threw up one hand. "I'll need another weapon. Mine was in my bag."

"Mercier will have things lined up by the time we get there."

He shrugged as if it didn't matter. "You look great! I hit the downstairs shops too. What do you think?" He held out his arms. "Look European enough?"

He wore a gorgeous cable-knit sweater, dark brown cords and Italian loafers. She almost salivated. "You'll do," she said.

He tossed a new leather jacket on the foot of her bed. "Dani, if you're upset about—"

She laughed. "Upset? No, of course not. Simple *lay* during a *lay*over. You know as well as I do how these things happen. Nothing to be upset about. Forget it."

"Forget it…"

His eyes narrowed, making him look sort of dangerous. But after a few seconds, his features evened out. He glanced out the window. "Are we set to go yet?"

Dani nodded. "We can leave for the airport anytime. The plane should have landed by now. As soon as it's serviced and we get clearance to take off, we can fly."

She sat on the edge of the bed and pulled on the low-heeled suede boots that matched her new brown wool pantsuit. She knew she looked professional. That was important today. Strictly business. No fancy makeup or hairdo or accessories.

Mercier hadn't said who would be joining them for the flight to Switzerland, but she had her bet on Cate. If there was anyone Dani did not want to recognize her burgeoning feelings for Ben Michaels, it was Cate. There would be no end to the jokes and everyone, including Jack, would have the whole story within hours. Unfortunately, feelings were virtually impossible to hide from Cate. She was a tad too telepathic for comfort.

Dani had to admit there was another reason she didn't want it to be Cate, a wholly inappropriate reason. Cate was a long-legged blond Nordic beauty who would look smashing next to Ben Michaels.

And maybe *to* Ben Michaels, as well. Jealousy was a new and unwelcome flea, one Dani hoped she could catch and pinch the life out of. She couldn't have Ben and that was a fact. Therefore, she shouldn't care who else had him, right? Right.

"We'll have some help. Mercier said he's sending another member of the team," she informed him.

Ben took the small bag she had purchased and headed out. She pulled the door closed behind her, determined to keep everything on a totally professional level from here on out. Maybe she would even fix Ben up with Cate. That would solve all her problems, now wouldn't it? It would prove how in control she was.

Her gaze followed him as he strode down the hallway to the elevators, unaware of her fixation on his back. On his wide shoulders and his narrow waist and his fine tush. She loved his relaxed gait, and how he could switch to that powerful stride when the situation called for it. He just exuded confidence and capability. And sex.

Dani squeezed her eyes shut and shook her head. Oh, man, she had it *so* damn bad and it was only going to get worse. She had to *do* something.

They boarded the small private jet Mercier sent for them. Ben saw they had company on the flight. Not realizing the other agent was *this* close, he had hoped they would have the plane to themselves.

She had been willing. More than willing, actually. And now she was acting as if it didn't matter at all. She sure didn't want to discuss it, he knew that much. He did. But not with that blonde present. She was already shooting him and Dani sly, curious looks, as if she could guess what their problem was.

"Cate Olin, Ben Michaels," Dani said, her words clipped.

Olin stuck out her hand to greet him. "Hi, Ben. Welcome aboard." She raised a finely shaped eyebrow at Dani. "I hear you two have been pretty busy. Want to catch me up?"

"Ben will fill you in," Dani said, sounding distracted. "I need to call Jack to let him know we're on our way."

"No need," Olin told Dani. "I just informed him you two were boarding and we would be off directly."

Dani shrugged. "Well, I need to ask him about the assets that will be available. So if you'll excuse me…"

"Oh, Jack sent all the info about that. It's in my briefcase." Olin grinned, rubbing her hands together with obvious anticipation. "Hope we get a few days R and R out of this. Maybe we can get in some slope time after we finish the op."

She took her seat in a dark gray padded recliner and gestured for Ben to sit facing her. "Do you ski, Ben?" she asked.

The tension had grown thick. Dani was ticked

off for some reason. And Cate Olin seemed to find that amusing.

"I was born on skis," he said in answer to Cate's question.

She laughed. "Your mother must have loved that experience!"

Ben smiled, then noted the tightening of Dani's lips. She was not amused. Did the two women not get along? he wondered. "How about you, Dani? You like to ski?"

"No," she said succinctly. "Never had the pleasure."

"I'll bet Ben would teach you," Cate said, a teasing note in her voice. The sound of the plane's engines distracted her. "Here we go. Everybody buckled up?"

They hadn't been in the air a half hour when Ben realized that Dani was trying to throw him together with Cate Olin. And that she was doing so reluctantly. When Cate excused herself later in the flight, he decided to nip this in the bud.

"What do you think you're doing?" he asked her.

Dani's eyes widened in a sorry attempt at innocence. "What do you mean?"

"I mean the obvious references to my lifestyle and your take on Cate's long-held dream of small town life. And the crack about the gross factor of sushi and how she and I both love it. You're going a little overboard pointing out our commonalities, don't you think? I've never appreciated being set up. Especially by someone I just— *What's* your motive?"

She shrugged, still giving him that doe-eyed, clueless look. "You seemed to have a lot in common, that's all. What's the matter? Don't you like Cate?"

Ben settled back and crossed his arms over his chest, glaring at her. "She's okay, but I don't get this. It's not as if you need to unload me on her to get rid of me."

He watched her shoulders slump a little as she shook her head. "No, it's not that."

"Then what?" He unclasped his arms and leaned forward.

"Just a little misdirection," she said in a near whisper, glancing guiltily at the aft section where Cate had gone, ostensibly to the restroom in the rear of the plane. "The boss thinks—" She broke off, took a deep breath and gave him a stony half smile. "Well, he somehow got the idea that I have a personal interest in you."

"But you don't," he said, feeling the sting. "So what's the difference in *you* having this interest and *Cate* having this interest?"

Dani rolled her eyes as if he should already know the answer. "Everybody knows Cate's would be temporary!"

"And yours wouldn't?" he asked.

"No, no, that's not what I meant." She blew out a harsh breath. "Just forget it."

"Highly unlikely if you keep playing match-maker." Ben didn't believe for a second that Dani's job was in danger because of this. It wasn't as if he were a suspect or a fellow agent. There were no rules that said they couldn't be involved if they happened to make a connection. No, it was that Dani's feelings for him made *her* uncomfortable. Fair enough. His for her shook him up more than a little, too.

Maybe he ought to encourage her to continue with the game. If he were the least bit drawn to Cate Olin, he might, but he wasn't. Not that Cate wasn't gorgeous, probably more classically beautiful than Dani. But something about Dani just set him on fire.

"Tell you what," he said, trying to look as serious as he possibly could. "I'm not looking to hook up with anybody right now. We'll keep everything on a strictly platonic level, all *three* of us, okay?"

"Great! Yes, if we could just do that. See, the, uh, what happened sort of threw me. I thought maybe you…well, never mind. I'm just glad we got this straightened out and that you agree. Thank you, Ben."

"Don't mention it," he said with an amiable nod.

"Don't mention what?" Cate said as she sailed back to the seating area and plopped down in her recliner. Her blue eyes were bright and her smile even brighter as she looked from one to the other. "What'd I miss?"

Ben faced her directly, his expression deadpan. "I just told Dani to stop trying to fix us up. You obviously don't need the help and I'm pretty much hung up on somebody else."

Cate laughed out loud, a full-throated laugh that was contagious. "Oh, God, the man's direct as death, isn't he?"

"Hung up on *who?*" Dani demanded, frowning at him.

Cate held up one long finger, "Uh, uh. Shouldn't that be *on whom?* Object of a preposition and all that?"

Ben nodded, his lips pursed. "I believe you're right, Cate. On *whom* sounds better anyway."

Dani threw up her hands, shot them a look of exasperation, marched into the aft cabin and shut the door.

"You're crazy about the girl, aren't you, Michaels?" Cate asked, grinning.

Ben inclined his head. "Isn't that obvious?"

"As I said, you are direct." She shook a lazy finger in his direction. "But I like you, Michaels, so I'm probably going to let you have your way."

Ben smiled. "Why do I sense there's a condition attached to that?"

Cate's cocky grin vanished. "You can play, but you have to be playing for keeps, that's all. If you don't play fair, I'll have to break off something important. And we're not talking fingers."

"I admire your loyalty, Cate, and I know Dani deserves it. I wish I could give you the assurance you're asking for."

"So what's the holdup?"

He shrugged. "Dani doesn't want this thing between us to go any further. She's made that clear. And I promised her I'd back off, so strictly business from here on out."

Cate laughed again, this time a bit more subtly than before. She shook her head. "Idiot. You act like you two have a choice."

Ben leaned forward, his elbows on his knees and his hands clasped between them. "Dani does have a choice, Cate, and I believe she's already made it."

She wore an expression of concern that looked out of place on her sophisticated features. It seemed almost motherly. "She had a premonition about you?"

"What do you mean, a premonition? About what?"

"Never mind," Cate said, breaking eye contact.

The whole situation was ridiculous. He wanted Dani, she wanted him. Why couldn't they just act on it and let all the peripheral problems take care of themselves? Where had his daring gone? Had it disappeared along with his familiar face?

His injuries had made him all too aware of the impact he had on others, that's what it was. He had seen firsthand and in detail how his mother had suffered because of the way he had lived his life. And not just her, either. His patient, loving father had borne the brunt of both their disabilities for well over a year and was bearing it still with his mother. Like it or not, Ben knew he must take everything into consideration when developing a relationship or anything else in his life. Coming on this mission was a mistake he should never have made. Falling for Dani, another mistake in the making.

"Always finish what you start, Michaels," Cate Olin said, her voice as commanding as her look.

Ben squinted at her. "Read minds, do you?"

She smiled, but her blue eyes were serious as a war. "Easily, so be careful what you think."

Ben would have laughed, but he had a sneaking suspicion there was no joke there.

"So you read minds and Danielle has premonitions. Must make some interesting investigations for that merry little band of yours."

She crossed her long, long legs and tapped her slender fingers on the arms of her chair. "Something tells me you're a skeptic, Michaels. Am I right?"

Ben smiled. "Do I need to answer or will you just read what's in here?" He tapped his head.

Her next smile seemed real. "Ah, well, I expect you'll come around in time. Dani's a little shy about broadcasting her talents so I won't elaborate on them, but I feel it's only fair to warn you about mine."

"Am I gonna get a parlor trick here to prove your point?" Ben asked.

She shrugged and closed her eyes. "If you insist. You were recently thinking how your involvement will affect your parents, your mother in particular. You plan to return home hale and hearty or in a box with a flag over it, not maimed as you were before, right? And you're concerned that they will have to worry about Dani, too, if you fall for her and they come to love her."

Ben's breath caught in his throat.

She flapped one long hand in a negligent wave of dismissal. "Child's play to read you. Believe me, nobody on the team's going to encourage your interest in Dani, Ben. We wouldn't want to lose her to Smalltown, America. And I seriously doubt you'd stir yourself up to join her in what she's doing. You'd love to, but you can't."

Ben didn't quite know what to say so he said nothing. He was even trying to keep his mind blank, he realized.

"Don't worry," Cate told him. "I promise not to dig around in your thoughts unless I think it concerns me or the operation. Or Dani, of course. I can turn it off and on at will."

"I see," he said simply. "I wonder…"

"If our paranormal proclivities are why we were hired for COMPASS?" she asked before he could say more. "In a word, yes. But we also have to qualify in all the usual areas. Have to excel, actually."

"So, all of you…" Ben made a rolling motion with his hand.

"All of us," she admitted. "Dani has premonitions. I'm telepathic. Vanessa has what we like to call 'cat sense.' She manages to land on her feet no matter what. No real category for that yet, but it's been real handy."

"All women on your squad?" he asked.

"Well, there's our control, Mercier. Plus one other guy." She paused, playing with the catch on her seat belt as she spoke. "I guess I don't have to tell you this information is not for public knowledge."

Ben laughed. "Like anybody would believe me! So, how do you plan to use these gifts to help us on this op?"

"However I can."

Dani returned with a tray bearing three cups. "Coffee?"

"—tea or me?" Cate added, laughing. "I told him."

"I heard," Dani said, bending a little so Ben could reach his coffee. "Milk, no sugar, right?"

He nodded. "Do you mind my knowing? Why didn't you tell me yourself?"

She turned her back as she handed Cate her coffee, then set down the tray and took her own cup. When she was seated, she gave him a steady look. "I'll go you one better and tell you how I got the way I am. We might as well get everything out in the open so there won't be any further distractions."

Ben fanned his hands out. "I'm all ears."

She nodded, shot Cate a look, then faced him again. "Since the three of us already know we've been fighting sexual attraction, there's no point in treating it like it doesn't exist."

Ben shrugged. "Maybe you didn't notice, but I stopped fighting."

"Well, you have to know it's not a good idea. It would benefit us to get that out of the way for good so we can function efficiently. Telling you about myself is the best way to discourage any interest you have in me. Seeing your disgust will surely get rid of my interest in you."

"Disgust?" Ben asked with a laugh.

"Dani…" Cate said, like a warning.

"Fine then, here it is. I'm Rom. Gypsy."

"That's hardly disgusting. I'm sure there are many fine people among the Rom."

Maybe he was right. She didn't know any, fine or otherwise, except the two who had deserted her. "My mother was a palm reader. Father was an occasional carnival worker. Mostly he was a grifter. They were basically scam artists and thieves. Or what they prefer to call travelers."

"Okay," Ben said. "What happened?"

"While traveling through Iowa, they left us in the care of the state. We landed in an orphanage."

Ben nodded at her to go on. He didn't say so, but thought that she was probably lucky to have landed where she did, considering how far she had come in life since then.

She cleared her throat, glanced to Cate, possibly for support, and then continued. "Never heard from them again. Years later I waitressed my way through Iowa State, took a job with one of the forensic labs there and eventually got a masters."

Cate grinned. "Valedictorian and magna cum laude. Tell it like it is."

Dani blushed. "I went for criminal justice out of rebellion. Because the police and the Rom are natural enemies," she went on to explain.

Ben's expression said he was interested but not shocked.

"So that's the source of my so-called gift, a piddly leftover from Mommy's psychic proclivities. Turned off yet?"

Ben smiled. "Fascinated! All I inherited was the ability to function without a calculator."

Cate clapped her hands in glee. "This is *so* much better than TV."

Dani looked confused. "Ben, you don't understand. My people were *thieves*. Grifters."

Ben wished he could show her how little he cared about that. "And the old nature versus nurture question pops up, huh? Some of my ancestors were transported from England for theft. Some were already here and went after their scalps. We all have ancestral skeletons to rattle, Dani. Who cares, really? You're not them, and race surely doesn't determine anything. I'm pretty sure you're not a thief, given our mission here."

Cate chimed in, caught up in the moment, "Yeah, surely you don't think Mercier would have hired you for the team without a thorough background check. We had to vote you in, you know, so he shared it—"

Dani shot her a frown. "What do you *mean?*"

Dumbfounded, Dani gaped at her. "I never knew he…"

Cate glanced at Ben who urged her wordlessly to continue. "Read your file if you want the details. Picture two illiterate kids roaming around the country with toddlers, living hand to mouth, getting work where they could, stealing when they couldn't. There was an arrest and you and your sister went into the system, just as you remember. Your parents were allowed to say goodbye, then taken away. It was a minor theft, simple burglary, so they were released after serving a couple of months. But they simply didn't have the wherewithal or the education necessary to find and get you back. There's some evidence they tried… You're gonna have to forgive that failure, Dani."

Dani shuddered, her gaze fixed on her friend. "Are…are they still living?"

"Your mother died within the year. She must have suspected she was very ill before you were separated. Your father simply disappeared after that. No one knows what happened to him. He had lost the woman he considered his wife, his two children, and he had nothing else."

Dani looked distraught, suddenly fragile. "No... nobody told me. Why?" Ben went to her and put an arm around her, rubbing her back, smoothing her hair. She didn't object. She seemed numbed by the new information.

"We thought you knew." Cate got up and collected their cups, leaving them alone.

Dani ran a hand through her hair and shot Ben a look of defeat. "I should have looked into it."

She obviously needed time to absorb all this. "Why don't you take a break, Dani? I'm speaking here as a *friend*."

She nodded, looking terribly weary. "I think I'll go back there and try to get some sleep."

"Good idea," Ben said, giving her one last hug. She needed a friend right now, not a lover. "I'm sorry about your parents," he said. "At least now you know they didn't give you up by choice."

Her smile was weak, but she nodded. "Thank you, Ben. For that and the hugs. Sorry you had to listen to all this...personal stuff." She shrugged one shoulder. "I only wanted you to believe..."

"They gave you that gift, Dani, so they didn't leave you without some part of them."

Ben watched her go. He wasn't certain he bought

into the premonition thing. But he had been to death and back, and you didn't venture that far without learning there's more to life than science could ever explain.

Chapter 12

Dani wept a little for the parents she could scarcely remember. Maybe they had cared. Maybe they thought she and Carol would be better off without them. Hopefully they were together now and in a better place than the cold world that had treated them so sadly.

She could not understand how blasé Ben was about it all. Maybe he didn't mind her parentage, but she'd bet his mother would have a cow if she knew her little Benji was consorting with a Gypsy. *Consorting*. There was a great word.

The thought made her smile in spite of sadness.

Cate and the others knew her story. None of them had ever discussed it or seemed to care.

Maybe she made too much of it herself. At any rate, it was good to have it out in the open and not have to worry that Ben would find out later and hate her for lying by omission. If there was a later.

It wouldn't matter if they went their separate ways. Since when had the *ifs* sneaked in there? They would part. For sure.

She managed to sleep for an hour. She was too curious about what Cate and Ben were finding to discuss to stay out of the main cabin for long. They had plans to make before they landed.

When she entered the cabin, Ben was laying down a hand of cards. "Gin." He looked up at her. "Hi. You okay?"

Dani nodded and smiled at him. Nobody beat Cate at cards unless she let them. "What gives here?" Dani asked.

Cate grinned and collected the deck, shuffled expertly, then fanned them. "I played fair and he beat me. Goes to show you how stupid it is to play fair."

"Right," Ben agreed. "Use every edge you've got, I always say. Want to play a little poker?"

"With you counting cards? Get out," Cate said with a laugh. "Play with *her*. I'm going to wash up. We'll be landing shortly. You all want to go directly to the bank when we get there?"

They nodded in unison. "Might as well get the show on the road," Ben said. He glanced at his watch. "Should be there around four. Tell me it's not one of their bank holidays."

"Not," Cate assured him.

Dani knew they were giving her space to deal with this new knowledge about her past. They wouldn't bring it up again. Instead they were offering her the major distraction of getting down to work. "We should move in a hurry," she said.

"Are they aware of what we need?" Ben asked.

"Jack's already made contact and says they'll cooperate," Cate said. "They will provide records of the transactions if we prove the crime first. You know what sticklers they are for secrecy. I have the tape of the forced transfer at your bank."

Cate patted his arm. "It has audio. And I have a fax of the transaction that took place in the Cayman's transferring everything to Geneva. That'll be enough to freeze the funds, if the money's still there."

Dani held up a hand. "Ben thinks it might have been withdrawn and converted already into something less traceable and more easily transported, like maybe diamonds. They've might have had time if the deal with a seller was already agreed on."

Cate looked thoughtful. Then she shook that finger at them. "So what we'll be after is the one who withdrew it. That photo I will have before the bank closes. Count on it."

Ben nodded. "I'll try to pinpoint any major diamond deals soon as we get to the hotel and I can set up to hack a little."

Dani knew her duty. "I'll coordinate with the local authorities immediately. Also, we'll need clearance to carry weapons, two cars, maps and so forth. No rest for the weary."

Cate fiddled in her briefcase and handed Dani a small stack of notes. "Here's the skinny on the assets if you want to look it over before we land."

Dani thumbed through the lists. "Things are moving like clockwork so far. But there's always a fly in the ointment."

Cate rolled her eyes and inclined her head toward Ben. "Get used to her bad homilies and mixed metaphors."

His gaze turned her way. "I hadn't noticed that. There's truth in the trite and reassurance in repetition."

Cate laughed. "And where did that quote come from?"

"From me," he answered, giving Dani a conspiratorial wink. "So, we have our ducks in a row?"

Dani wanted to kiss him so badly her lips ached. "Ready to hit the ground running," she said instead.

* * *

Their jet landed at precisely four in the afternoon. Cate, eager to reach the bank before it closed, took a taxi. Dani headed for the Ariel car rental where Jack Mercier had arranged by phone for transportation.

The auto proved to be a lower end luxury model, one good for high speeds and absolute reliability. She got behind the wheel; Ben didn't object. He simply opened the map and began studying it so he could play navigator.

"Ever been to Switzerland?" Dani asked.

"No, but it's awesome, isn't it? Flying in was a real experience." He had gazed out at the mind-boggling scenery that swept past during their entry.

The classically elegant Hotel Bellevue Palace was a five-star and located next to the Swiss parliament building. Their rooms had breathtaking views.

Jack had arranged for only two rooms, putting her in with Cate. No surprise there. The place was expensive and the COMPASS budget, while generous, was not without limit. Dani wondered if Jack thought he was doing her a favor by providing her with a chaperone.

She showered, changed into black wool slacks, a matching sweater and comfy flats. Then she went next door and found Ben already at his computer, tapping away. "Find anything yet?"

He turned and gave her a warm smile, seeming to

like what he saw. She liked her view, too. He wore gray flannel slacks and a black flat-knit shirt with the sleeves pushed to his elbows. His forearms were strong, sexy even. His dark hair glistened, still damp from a shower.

"How's it going?" she asked.

He got up, walked slowly over to her and put his arms around her. No groping or grasping, simply a gentle hug that felt wonderfully sweet. He nuzzled her neck just below her ear, then buried his face in her hair, inhaling deeply. She knew it smelled of plain old coconut shampoo and suddenly wished she wore perfume.

Dani reminded herself that she shouldn't want to entice him, not with perfume or anything else. She remained still, trying not to do something really stupid.

"Just needed a little human warmth. You mind?" he asked.

Dani moved a little closer. "N-no. It's okay."

Without comment, he released her and turned back to the screen. "I started with the Persand company. Hacked into the CEO's private e-mail. Found several interesting messages directed to Liechtenstein. They might be going after stamps instead of diamonds."

Dani quirked her eyebrow. "Postage stamps?"

"Smart conversion," he muttered. "You all have any assets to draw on in Liechtenstein?"

"You're kidding, right? The country's not much *larger* than a postage stamp. As far as I know, we have had no dealings there...but they are a part of NATO. I'm sure we can get cooperation. You know much about stamps?"

Ben shrugged. "Not a lot, but I'm learning fast." He nodded at the screen. "The ones inquired about are apparently extremely rare."

"Easy to trace then," Dani said hopefully.

"Not necessarily. Private collectors play it pretty close to the vest. Converting stamps back to cash would be a piece of cake when funds were required. Easy to transport to anywhere in the world."

A knock on the door interrupted his thoughts.

"You order room service?" Dani asked.

"No."

Drawing her weapon, she pushed him to one side of the door frame and moved to the other. Loudly, she demanded, "Who is it?"

"Cate."

Both exhaled a little breath. Ben opened the door and stood aside. "So, how did it go?"

She presented him with a folder and smiled. "I always get my man. Bertrand Nicollier is our bank contact and he was very helpful. Mercier's influence is widespread and impressive."

Dani watched as Ben opened the folder.

Cate tapped the page. "We have a face. We have a name."

Ben spread out the information beside his laptop on the table. It consisted of several stills from the bank's video, a form with the client's information and a signed document of withdrawal.

Ben nodded thoughtfully. "You know, that's not a lot of backing, but it could still create major havoc. It's not as if 9/11 required a tremendous amount of money. Cate, you said you have photos from the Cayman bank that Mercier e-mailed you? I need to see them."

Cate produced another envelope from her briefcase. Ben opened it and studied the contents. With a shake of his head, he exhaled sharply and sat. "Okay, it's making more sense now."

"And what have you deduced?" Cate asked.

Ben sighed. "Might as well have a seat. This is not a short story." He massaged his forehead as if it pained him suddenly.

"What about the stamps?" Dani asked. "Aren't we in a rush?"

He motioned to the phone. "You need to get your COMPASS resources busy locating and tracking this guy," he said, thumping one of the photos. "They can do it faster than we can. We can intercept him after the buy if you intend to make the bust."

"You recognize him?" Cate asked, pulling one of the photos over to her.

"He's Andros Kelior," Ben said. "Served with me in Afghanistan." He produced the grainy video still that Jack Mercier had gotten from the bank in Grand Cayman. "And this is Ace Belken. He was there, too. I'd like to think he drowned when that boat flipped off Grand Cayman, but I'd bet my last nickel he survived, at least for a while. Somebody had to alert Kelior that we had escaped and send him to Toronto to bomb our flight."

"What does this mean, Ben?" Dani asked. "That all this has nothing to do with terrorist activities? That the theft was directed at you? At your bank?"

"Oh, it has to do with terror, all right," he told her. He touched his thumb to his forefinger. "First order of business is this. A front man is selected, someone who could be seen by the others as dedicated to jihad. Enter Andros Kelior. His father is Greek, but his mother is Iranian. He has the family connections and the contacts. We used that in our missions, and now he's using it for his own purposes."

"A traitor. You don't think he's in charge of this, though, do you?" Dani guessed.

Ben shook his head. "No, I'm pretty sure I know who's running the show. Now then, Kelior contacts all the other clients I had with sympathetic Middle Eastern ties and hits them up for funds for the cause of jihad. He promises them he has the perfect way to take their money, put it to use, *and* to get them reimbursed for it, to boot. Wouldn't they just love the irony? Even if these donors aren't all that inclined to give up the good life they've been living in the U.S., they can contribute without detection or loss and still get underground credit for supporting the jihad."

"Their money's insured, so they aren't out anything, yeah," Dani said. "Go on."

He ticked off on another finger. "Get another fellow, this one a true son of al Qaeda, the Taliban or whatever arm of Satan he's chained to. He has to be expendable and not wise to the big picture. That would be the guy who hit my bank. His motive is moving the money to finance the cause. Period. Got it?"

Cate and Dani nodded.

"Doesn't matter that he dies in the process, except that those in control will have to replace him if they want to do a repeat performance. His only job was to get the money where it was intended to go, the Cayman bank. That, and to help lay the blame on me."

Ben tapped a third finger. "Waiting there is Ace Belken. He's supposed to move the funds out of the Cayman bank. He takes his cut and sends the rest to Switzerland to another account in the name of the bogus company."

"But Fontenot was on to him," Dani guessed.

Ben nodded. "The move was suspicious to say the least. At the last minute, the brains behind the plan notifies Belken that I'm still alive and following the money. He knows me and would have been waiting for me to show up in the Caymans. He must have been watching the hotel and saw us heading for the boat. He and whoever was riding shotgun for him came after us, but not before he called Kelior as a failsafe—bomb onboard our plane in case we manage to get past Belken and try to fly over here."

He shook his head. "Kelior could easily have beaten us to Toronto if he flew directly from the States. He was Explosive Ordnance, the man with the right experience. He could have rigged the bomb easily and slipped it in that kid's bag."

Cate blew out a soft whistle. "And now he's here, this Andros Kelior."

Ben went on, his voice hard. "Persand manufactures antiterrorist gear. Weaponry, vests, even owns several security companies that supply personnel. The terrorists act, the government reacts. They pay Persand to supply what they need. And they pay a hell of a lot more than three million. Of course, Persand doesn't even pay that. Federal insurance does." He slapped a hand on the desk, then fisted it. "Persand's CEO is behind it all. That he gets my hide in the bargain is just chocolate on his cake. I could have been killed in the bank robbery, or, if I lived, I was set up to be implicated in all this. A personal side bar to his main plan."

"You! It sounds like traitorous, big business greed to me! You still think this is personal?" Dani asked.

He got up, paced the carpet for a minute before answering. "I know it for a *fact*. I found out who Persand really is, who owns the company, when I first hacked into them in the Caymans. I just hoped there was some mistake, some explanation, that maybe he was being set up, too." He shook his head. "But with Kelior and Belken in on it, there's no doubt now who's in charge."

"Well, don't keep us in suspense. Who is it?" she demanded.

"The man who survived the same explosion I did in Afghanistan. Victor Bruegel. My lieutenant."

Cate's intense blue gaze locked on Ben. Dani could tell she had begun reading his every thought. "He wants you dead."

Ben nodded. "Not only dead. Obviously he wants me discredited, charged with theft, maybe even treason. The question is *why?*" He pounded a fist in his palm. "I *trusted* him. He was a good officer."

He sighed, a rough sound, pained. Then he walked over to the window and looked out at what would have been a magnificent view. But Dani knew Ben didn't even see the snow-covered peaks, the thousand shades of evergreen, the city below. His voice was barely audible when he said, "This has something to do with what happened on that last mission. But for all three of them to be involved…"

Cate nudged Dani and with just the barest shake

of her head indicated Dani shouldn't start an inquisition. She glanced at the door, a silent suggestion that they leave Ben alone for a while.

Dani wasn't about to desert him when he was obviously upset by betrayal. She knew that horrible hurt, had felt it, too. He knew those men, had served with them. Why were they trying to destroy him?

Cate grasped her arm and duck-walked her to the door.

"Meet us downstairs in the restaurant in an hour, Ben. We'll discuss this in more detail and file an interim report right after dinner," Cate said as she firmly shoved Dani through the door.

"What are you doing?" Dani protested, yanking her arm out of Cate's grasp. "We can't just leave him like that!"

"You have to." Cate roughly turned her toward their room and put a hand in her back to hurry her along.

Dani only resisted a little, just on principle. Cate towered over her by nearly a foot and outweighed her by a good thirty pounds. Also, her senses had put her inside Ben's head just now, so she would know if he wanted them gone.

"You're telling me he has to work through it. Alone?"

Cate ran her key card through the slot and stood aside for Dani to enter their room. "He's trying to decide how to handle things. He knows these men and we don't. He just needs a little space to work out the details without you asking a bunch of questions." She quirked her head, causing her straight blond locks to settle over one eye. Impatiently, she raked it back. "You love this guy."

Dani scoffed as she flopped down on the nearest bed. "Go *ahead*. Read my mind."

"Careful how you throw that invitation around, kiddo. But I'm not about to internally manage your love life."

"Ha!" Dani exclaimed with a bitter laugh. "Pull the other leg. You intrude all the time. You were reading Ben's mind like a TelePrompTer, and don't tell me you weren't!"

Cate sat beside her on the bed and slapped her on the knee. "Listen, honey. That man's hauling a truckload of baggage you can't even hope to help him unload. Mercier's worried your maternal instincts will override your good sense."

"*Maternal?* Give me a break. Ben's got enough mama at home for several guys. I never cast a maternal thought in his direction, believe me."

"Protective instincts, then. You want to fix his problems for him, Dani, and you can't." She sighed. "Look, I like Ben. A lot. He's a great guy, but maybe not great for you."

"Why not for me?" Dani demanded.

"You're both control freaks for one thing." She grinned.

Dani shrugged that off, unwilling to argue against the truth. Instead, she asked, "So what's the matter with him otherwise? What is the problem that I can't help him with?"

Cate explained. "Ben's still feeling guilt over that suicide bomber mission in Afghanistan, even though he knows everything he did then was justified. He'll come to terms with that eventually. It's his life now that's really giving him fits. He might or might not be able to reconcile the changes he's undergone, how his way of *being* has had to change. But he needs to do that and you can't help him. So, cool it while you still can."

She paused. "*If* you still can."

Cate was right. Mercier was right. But Dani kept feeling Ben's pain of betrayal. And remembering, too, the incredible connection between their two bodies. She could still feel the sensuous glide of his long, strong hands over her body as they had embraced in that river of temptation heated by the earth's very core. And the greater warmth soon after.

Cool it, Cate had said, while she still could. Dani threw an arm over her eyes to block out the light from the window. And maybe in a naive effort to prevent her friend from entering further into her thoughts. As if that would work.

"All right then," Cate said, sounding resigned as she rose from the bed and headed for the bathroom.

Dani didn't know what she meant by that and didn't ask. Was Cate giving up or had she simply decided to back off with the mind reading? Not that it mattered. What would be, would be.

Dani let her thoughts drift where they would, touching on her feelings for Ben and skipping to her perpetual need for a closeness with another she had never quite reached. Until Ben.

Maybe he would be able to look past who and what she was, but could she ever be certain just who and what *he* was? Did he even know himself? The banker image he had forced himself into didn't fit.

Dani willed her thoughts away from Ben. She needed to concentrate on the very present problem of the money scheme and what it all meant.

For the moment, however, she cleared her mind of even that. The past couple of days had been too hectic. She sought calm in the mantra that had seen her through crises before.

This, too, shall pass. This, too, shall pass.

It didn't seem to be working. The harder she tried to relax, the worse the tension grew.

A gradual sense of foreboding rippled through her body as she lay there. Danger creeping in on cat's feet. Her entire being began to thrum with it.

But was it personal, involving the loss of her heart

to a man who might break it? Or was it physical? Had this enemy of Ben's somehow discovered their location again?

"Cate?" she called as she sat up and tried to zero in on the source of her premonition. On whatever details she could capture.

The pressure grew strong, very strong this time. Light flashed like a strobe behind her eyelids, granting her momentary glimpses. Horrible frames. Scary. Her muscles tightened painfully, her senses sharpening to a knife's edge.

Dani smelled cordite. Heard deafening reports of gun fire. A metallic, coppery taste flooded her mouth and nose. Her fingers grasped the comforter beneath her, squeezing fabric soaked in gore.

Things to come!

Breath stalled in her throat until she forced in a draught of needed oxygen and expelled it with a terrible cry.

Chapter 13

Victor Bruegel slammed the phone down and paced his office like a caged beast. What was wrong with Kelior? He hated inefficiency. He hated failure. He hated Ben Michaels—the man must have nine lives!

Sucking in a deep breath, he calmed his fury as best he could. If he wanted this done, he might have to do it himself. Maybe that was why those he had hired couldn't seem to succeed. Maybe *he* was meant to do it.

How simple it would have been to have Michaels destroyed as he had lain helpless in the hospital after the mission. A mistake not to move on him then, but it had seemed that letting him live would be the greater punishment. Man without a face. Man without his former abilities. Man without his pride. But that man had surprised everyone, especially Victor. He had recovered and now had a better life than ever before. The outrageous injustice of that could not be tolerated.

Killing him should be enough, but destroying his reputation, his family's honor and any fond memories anyone might hold of him was still possible. Everything was set up—it had taken a monumental effort on Victor's part. Hell, he'd had to consort with all kinds of scum to arrange this. Getting full control of Persand and making the necessary contacts had taken nearly a year. Besides, if Michaels screwed this arrangement Victor had made with the Servants of Al Muhad, heads would roll. One of them Victor's.

Yes, he would have to handle this. This last botched attempt, the survival of Flight 3271, was surely a sign.

He picked up the phone again and instructed his assistant to get him reservations on the next flight to Frankfurt, where he had legitimate business to conduct. From there he would drive to Geneva.

Victor smiled to himself now that the decision was made. Yes, this felt exactly right. No doubt Michaels would actually be glad to see him, would probably even ask for Victor's help.

"And I will help you, you son of a bitch," Victor said, his lips stretching into a mirthless grin. "I will help you right into hell."

Cate came running naked from the bathroom, her weapon in her hand.

Dani was already up and stepping into her shoes. She glanced up. "Just got a helluva premo. Something's going down. Grab some clothes and meet me in Ben's room."

Cate disappeared back into the bathroom as Dani hurried next door. "It's Dani—let me in!" she called as she rapped on it.

The door flew open and Ben stood there looking confused. She pushed past him. "Close the door but stay there. Cate will be here in a minute." She wondered if he would credit her vision when she told him about it.

"What's up?" he asked, running a hand through his hair and bringing it back down to rest on his bare chest. His eyes looked tired. She noted again the numerous healed scars on his body that she had first seen when they swam together, and again in bed. Some were like burns, some were long incisions.

He saw her looking and traced one with his finger. "You could have asked. Truck was bombed. Shrapnel here," he said easily. "Neat ones are balloon grafts, used to rebuild the face."

Dani watched his features again, seeing it with new eyes. Perfect plastic surgery.

"I wasn't always this pretty," he joked with a wry smile.

Dani smiled. Trying to subdue her jangling nerves, she joked back, "Six Million Dollar Man. I've heard of you."

"A slight exaggeration. What's the matter, Dani?" he asked. "You're not yourself."

Dani sighed and leaned against the wall. "Tell you in a minute. No point repeating. I haven't explained it to Cate yet."

"Are you all right?" he demanded. He started to reach out to her, then seemed to think better of it and propped his hand on his hip.

Dani's gaze followed automatically, landing on his bare waist where his pants rode low. His abs were spectacular. Not an ounce of spare flesh. She nodded, biting her bottom lip impatiently. "I'm *okay*. Where the *hell* is Cate?"

A sharp knock answered that question. Ben let her in then ushered the two toward some chairs and a table by the window. He plopped down on the rumpled bed, not demanding answers but simply waiting expectantly.

She took a deep breath and met his eyes directly. "The shootout will take place in a room with lots of glass. A large room."

"What shootout?" Ben asked.

"The one in Dani's premonition. Maybe the bank?" Cate suggested.

"But you've already been there," Dani pointed out. "We won't need to go back there for anything, will we?"

Cate thought for a moment. "We might if something else comes up. They had quite a few windows in front." She glanced at Ben's laptop. "Boot up and see if they have a Web site with photos. Maybe Dani can tell if that's the place."

Ben looked puzzled, but got up to do as she said.

"I had a vision," Dani explained. "We were taking fire and returning it."

"Mmm-hmm," he said, busy logging on from his standing position between their chairs.

Dani's knees brushed his legs, they were so close. The urgent warning she had just experienced mixed with the buzz of arousal. Or perhaps caused it. She shifted in her chair, unable to stand still. The compulsion to *do* something zinged in her. She looked to Cate. *Help me explain! Make him hurry!*

Cate cleared her throat. "We have to take what she saw seriously, Ben. She's been right on the money too many times to ignore it. Nobody who knows her ignores it. It's one of the reasons Mercier took her for COMPASS."

"Okay," he said, inclining his head toward his laptop. "There you go. Banque Mureaux et Cie."

Dani and Cate gathered closer to look at the Web site as he clicked through it. "Only shows the facade," Cate said with a huff.

Ben cleared his throat. "Dani, is this confrontation supposed to take place soon?"

Dani shrugged. It was damn difficult not to sound hyper. "Usually things are fairly immediate, often almost instantaneous—but this didn't appear to be one of those times."

"I see," he said, his expression deadpan.

Did he see? Did he believe her or was he simply humoring her? Dani felt defensive. She had never much cared about skeptics before but she truly wanted *him* to credit her ability. "I need you to believe me, Ben," she said. "For your own good as well as ours, don't blow this off."

"I get that," he told her, nodding, but Dani sensed his doubt. Cate was rolling her eyes and looking frustrated. "What's your problem?" she asked him.

"It's not that I'm close-minded about it." He shook his head and stepped away from the computer, turning his back on them. "First, I haven't dealt with this ESP stuff much, ever, but I can't help asking myself why there were none of these episodes during the last couple of days." He gestured with both hands out. "Surprised by a gunman at the bank door. Armed thugs chasing us down by boat. Bomb on the plane. Seems to me these little warnings are mighty selective." He shrugged, palms upturned. "Gotta wonder why *now*."

Dani knew she had to keep calm, not blame him for his disbelief. His questions were perfectly valid. "I *did* have premonitions about every one of those. I just didn't relate them to you as that. They aren't real specific, and sometimes I confuse them with…other strong feelings."

"Like what?" he asked, squinting at her.

Dani ignored the question. She didn't want to tell him how her physical attraction to him distracted her. Who in her right mind would give a man *that* advantage? "I strongly suggested we leave the hotel immediately, didn't I? And I found the bomb on the plane, remember?"

He looked thoughtful. "Okay, I'll grant you that. But what about the initial robbery? And the boat thing. You jumped right on the boat with no hesitation."

Dani's lips tightened. She looked at Cate who also seemed very interested in the answer. "I ignored the uneasiness I felt when approaching the bank. Something, another stronger urge, had prompted me to go there in the first place. I guess that took precedence or something. To tell you the truth, even though there were a few hairy moments, I never really felt out of control."

"Well, good for you, Ms. Nerves of Steel," he drawled. "I was damn near petrified."

"No, you were mad as hell, I remember," Dani corrected. She took a breath and thought back to when they were leaving Grand Cayman. "As for the boat chase, I was already hyped from trying to get you to leave the hotel in a hurry. Maybe the premonitions overlapped. And they don't always involve *all* my senses."

She squeezed her eyes shut. "Like right now. I no longer see anything happening, but the hum of danger is steady after the initial vision. It will probably continue until something happens. The eventuality of it coming true will dispel it."

It was like that hum of arousal Ben caused, she knew, always there, increasing and decreasing in direct proportion to his nearness. Was that going to last until something else happened between them? If it would simply go away, maybe she could get a clearer picture of the danger they were in.

Dani could see he still didn't quite believe her, but at least he hadn't dismissed it all out of hand.

"Fine. So we stay locked and loaded from now on," he said, pursing his lips. "But we should do that anyway. I'll need a weapon. Can you arrange it?"

"Right. I'm on that now. Dani got us clearance," Cate said slowly, shooting Dani a what-can-you-do-with-the-idiot look. "I'm going down to get some food. You guys feel free to debate, bump uglies or whatever until you get hungry."

Ben ran a hand over his lower face, barely hiding a smile.

Cate could be crude. "I think he's through debating." She winked at Dani as she closed the door.

Dani knew she should go with Cate. Ben had been warned. And his room was not the location where she had seen the firing take place, so he should be safe enough.

He approached her, standing close, not touching. "I want to know more about these feelings," he said softly. "The ones that screw with the premonitions."

Dani's gaze slid away from his. "No you don't."

"But I do," he insisted. "Do they have to do with us? With the current bouncing back and forth between us?"

Her laugh was a little shaky. "Now you're as bad as Cate. Next you'll be suggesting we *bump uglies* to dispel the sparks."

He laughed. "Couldn't hurt."

"It could. You don't want to start something between us."

"It's already started," he said, his laugh dwindling to a sweet smile. He reached out, touched her arm and trailed one long finger down to her wrist, catching her hand in his. "See?"

The sensation of that light contact sent a flood of warmth straight to her center. "I'm afraid I don't do casual sex well."

He went from smile to serious regard. "I don't do casual sex at all."

Pure heat radiated from him, encompassed her and melted her reason. Dani wanted him so fiercely she almost threw herself into his arms. His perfect lips beckoned hers, irresistibly. Still, something warned her there would be no way she could take another taste of this pleasure and then give it up.

Bless him, he took away her choice and lowered his head to hers. She felt the warm firmness of his lips press her brow, glide to her temple, her cheek and come to rest on her mouth. Her lips opened ready and eager to accept.

He released her hand and slid his arms around her, pulling her close. Dani abandoned caution and rode the swell of desire building inside her. He pressed against her, creating an even greater need.

The kiss ended. Dani groaned in protest and sought his mouth again, her eyes still closed, her entire body alive with desire.

"What do you see for us, Danielle?" he whispered. His mouth lightly brushed hers. "What will happen next?"

Dani tried her best to control her breathing, to recover and give him some pithy reply to punish him for teasing her so. But what came out was the truth. "I see your mother ready to wring my neck and you being forced to take sides."

"You do not." His hands immediately dropped to his sides. There was suddenly an icy blank space between them where there had only been delicious heat before. "That's cold," he snapped.

"And *true*," she muttered, more or less to herself.

"You're actually saying you *see* this in that head of yours?" he demanded. "And you claim you want me to believe in your damned visions? You *don't* see that!"

Dani remained still, resolute. "No official premonition required for this one. It's already a law that guys like you don't bring home a Gypsy girl. I'm your parents' worst nightmare."

Dani opened her eyes and looked up at him. His teeth were clenched. A muscle worked in his jaw and there were faint new frown lines between his eyes. If nothing else, she was giving his new face character.

"That didn't enter your head, did it, Ben? Taking me home with you. But I tell you this and you can take it to the bank," she said, waving her finger under his nose. "I could never adapt to small town existence. And I surely don't intend to be your one last fling in the danger zone."

She moved to the door, feeling as if her feet were mired in setting cement. She had to get out of this room while she still could.

Ben didn't try to stop her.

Oh God, she prayed as she hurried down the hall to her room, *please don't let me break down and cry like a little girl.* She had not shed a tear over anything since she was twelve. Until she'd met him.

But when the door closed behind her, she leaned against it and put in an amendment to that prayer, mumbling the words out loud between sobs. "Okay, but please don't ever let him *see* me do it."

Chapter 14

Ben knocked softly on her door. When she refused to answer, he banged with his fist. "Dani? It's me. Open up."

He put his ear to the door and didn't hear a thing. Maybe she had gone downstairs to the restaurant where Cate was. He waited a few minutes, listening, then called out again. "Dani? Are you in there? Please. This is urgent."

Nothing. With a head shake and a sigh, he started to the elevators. Then he heard the dead bolt click and turned.

"What's happened?" she asked, her head down as

she closed the door and started down the hall toward him. "This had better be about the case."

He reached out to her but dropped his hand when she stepped back. "We have to straighten this out," he said. "We can't do what we have to do if we can't work together."

"Got that right," she muttered, adjusting the strap of her purse on her shoulder, still refusing to meet his eyes. Her voice sounded thick and pitched lower, as if she'd been crying. "But we're done talking about you and me, and we do *have to* go anyway. Cate will be waiting." She brushed past him, marched to the elevator and punched the button with a vengeance.

Someone had really done a job on her self-image, he thought. Some man's unaccepting family, no doubt.

Ben had to admit that his parents wouldn't be thrilled if he announced he was interested in her. Not for the reasons she thought, however. No, they simply wouldn't want him mixed up with anyone in her profession. That would just be somebody else they had to worry about dying.

The doors to the elevator opened and he stepped in behind her. "We'll work it out," he promised, accepting and then dismissing her angry glare. Her eyes were all red. He'd been right about the crying and it made him want to comfort her again. Like she would allow that.

He locked his hands behind him. "We'll talk again."

She shot him an angry look and pushed out ahead of him the instant the doors opened. He followed her as she strode forcefully in the direction of the hotel dining room.

Cate had a table by the huge picture windows looking out over the city. She stood and waved to get their attention.

Dani had made it halfway across the room when she abruptly stopped. Ben crashed into her back. She made a sound, half cry, half grunt, then turned and grabbed him, pulling them both to the floor. Shots rang out. Glass shattered. Bullets whizzed by them. Screams issued all around them as patrons over-turned tables and chairs in their haste to escape.

A patron's shoe ground Ben's hand into the carpet just as another clipped the side of his head. Mass panic. Ben grabbed Dani and rolled them under a table to keep from being trampled in the stampede.

She struggled against his grip, scrambled to her knees and was out from under cover before he could stop her. Helpless, he watched her back as she took a shooting stance, gun gripped with both hands and returned fire. Dammit, he was unarmed. Couldn't do a thing to help her. Another volley cleared the table next to him, showering him with glass and wine.

Dani continue to return fire and dropped again, one hand on his head, shoving him flat as she went down.

The firing had stopped. Either she had taken out

the shooter, he had fled or he was waiting for them to show themselves.

"Dani?" Cate called above the din of fleeing patrons.

Ben thought she sounded strange, her voice strained and high-pitched, totally unlike the woman who never seemed to lose her cool. Something was wrong.

He started to get up, but Dani grabbed him by the belt and yanked him back. "Stay low," she ordered, her words brusque.

Ben did as she said, crawling on his hands and knees over broken dishes, puddles of drinks and spilled food, snaking between upended tables and those still upright. It was combat all over again. Only this time, he was an unarmed civilian.

He trained his eyes on Dani's shapely behind which was right in front of him. She had lost her shoes in the scramble. Her bare feet looked vulnerable and small as she crawled toward Cate's table, fast as a baby on caffeine.

"Catie!" she cried. "You hit?"

"Yeah, a little."

A little? Either you were hit or you weren't. Ben scooted past Dani and reached Cate first. "Grab some clean napkins!" he ordered. "And get an ambulance here!"

A stack of folded cloth napkins landed in his hand. He stretched the V-neck of Cate's sweater off her shoulder. "Got a nick, maybe caught that tendon," he told her. He had seen plenty of gunshot wounds during his tour of duty and had patched up a few until the medics could get to them. Ben placed a pad of the cloths over the gash and applied pressure. "You'll be fine, Cate."

"Never saw him…too late," she muttered, closed her eyes and went limp.

"Cate?" He slid his free hand under her head and felt a wetness matting her thick blond mane. Maybe from a spill, he hoped. But when he checked his hand, blood.

"Dani?" he shouted, glancing over his shoulder.

She was gone, as were all the customers and staff in the place. He flashed back to the explosion that nearly took his own life. Alone again, except for a casualty. At least this time, he wasn't injured, too.

"Hang in there, Cate," he said. He heard the strident blare of sirens getting louder. "Help's on the way."

He didn't have to wonder where Dani was. She had gone after the shooter. Ben cursed under his breath, itching to follow her, but he couldn't leave Cate like this. Dani would never forgive him. And she could handle herself. He had to trust that she could because he didn't have any other choice.

"Medic!" he shouted when he heard a commotion just outside the dining room. "Over here!" He raised one bloodied hand and waved so they could locate him among the tables and chairs.

The instant he was certain Cate had the attention she needed, he dashed out of the dining room to look for Dani. He saw her almost immediately. She stood, gesturing wildly, obviously explaining the incident to the Swiss police. He hurried to join them.

"How's Cate?" she asked, interrupting her conversation with the officer.

"Shoulder wound, not serious. Head's bleeding. I probed a little but couldn't locate an entry wound. Her hair's really thick and I might have missed it. Maybe hit something when she fell. She lost consciousness."

"Oh, God," Dani said, exhaling sharply. They both looked around as Cate was rushed out to the ambulance. Dani turned her attention to the policeman. "We have to go. You need anything else, we'll be at the hospital."

They ran, barely making it to the ambulance before the doors were closed. Dani flashed her badge. "*Elle est l'un des nos agents.* She's one of ours," she told the paramedics, who made room for them to ride along.

"Did you get a look at the shooter?" Ben asked her as they squeezed inside.

She shook her head, grimacing as she watched one of the attendants tape down Cate's IV. "I think he's American."

The back doors of the ambulance slammed shut. "How could you tell?" Ben asked.

"I got one of his shoes," she said. "Maybe we can get prints."

"You got close enough to get his shoes?"

She shook her head again, never taking her eyes off Cate. "He outran me. One came off when he scrambled into the getaway car. Got the plates."

"Good work! The police have the shoe?" he asked as the vehicle tore into the street, its siren blaring.

Dani patted her bulging shoulder bag. Her lips were tight and her forehead creased with worry. He felt her pain as if it were his own.

She obviously hadn't seen the shooter before he opened fire and neither had Cate, according to what she had told him. Some things you just couldn't anticipate. He had learned that the hard way. But Dani thought she could. And that she *should*. She would blame herself if Cate didn't make it.

He put his arm around her and gave her a hug. It was not her fault, he wanted to say.

But how many people had insisted that *he* was in no way at fault for the deaths caused by that bomb? No way for him to know that the child had let himself be wired. Who is his right mind would believe a boy would destroy his own family just to kill a couple of Americans? Ben should have frisked him. Why hadn't he?

Not to blame, huh? *He* hadn't believed that for a minute before and neither would Dani now about herself.

"I have to stay with Cate." Dani handed Ben her cell phone. "Can't use this in here. Go and call

Mercier. Speed dial one. Give him this license number to trace." She rattled it off. "He'll give you a contact here. Can you lift prints?"

Ben shook his head.

"Okay, make the calls, let Mercier know the prints will be coming within the hour if I can get any off the shoe. Hurry back and sit with Cate while I do that. She has to be attended by one of us, even if there's surgery."

"I know the drill."

"I thought you might." Dani gave him a little push to hurry him along. Suddenly she remembered that Ben was a target, too. "Watch your back," she warned. "Don't go outside."

He shot her a look that said he was neither a child nor the village idiot. She shrugged an apology as he left and turned her attention to Cate. The doctor was examining the injury to her head and ordering her to X-ray. He turned to Dani as he ripped off his gloves. "Shoulder should be fine. It'll scar without stitches, but I think we should see about her head injury first. There's massive swelling and she's comatose."

"She was hit there, too?" Dani asked.

"Apparently she struck something sharp near the base of the skull."

"But she was lucid," Dani told him. "She called out to me. Talked to Ben."

He nodded. "A good sign, indicating that the

edema is the problem. When the swelling subsides, she should come out of it. Still, we need a scan to determine the extent of the damage." He pushed past her. "Excuse me."

Dani followed the gurney as they wheeled Cate to X-ray. Ben joined her in the hallway and handed her the phone she had given him. "Mercier's sending a local to attend Cate, be here in about a half hour. He's running that license and wants prints or partials ASAP if you can get any. Oh, and he ordered us to a safe house. Said you have the address."

As if she planned to hang around some hole in the wall when there was so much to do. "Go with Cate," Dani said. "If she says anything, write it down, make notes on who heard it."

"I *know*," he said. Dani frowned at his back as she stopped at the waiting area and he continued on down the hallway with the gurney. Cate had been right, they were both control freaks.

Right now she needed to get down to plain old police work.

She went to the receptionist at the window and flapped open her badge folder. "Please get me a small container of talcum powder," she said in French. "And give me your tape dispenser, would you?"

The young receptionist, looking a bit startled, did as she asked. "Thank you," Dani said with a smile. "Now, do you have any more of those slick black folders over there?" The girl nodded and opened a deep drawer full of supplies.

"An empty one, please, from the middle of the stack," Dani ordered. She held it by the edge when the girl handed her the item. Dani thanked her again and went back to her chair. She noted a few strange looks from six others in the waiting room as she withdrew the cheap, black men's shoe from her purse and carefully set it aside on the end table beside her chair.

Ignoring her audience, she found her small makeup bag and retrieved the camel-hair brush she used for her blusher.

Very carefully, Dani dusted the shoe with talc, smiling tightly as she discovered the splotches and began to lift them with the tape. She stuck pieces of tape to the shiny black surface of the file folder. "There," she muttered to herself. "Now to send."

With the receptionist glaring at her, she took out her satellite cell phone, used the photo option and quickly transmitted the images to Control. They would be of high enough resolution that the COMPASS computers could maybe approximate a match.

Mission accomplished, she closed the phone and tucked it away along with the shoe and her makeup bag. Sometimes she had to do things the quick way. The cops would have taken hours.

Just then a woman entered the waiting area.

"Danielle Sweet?" she asked, a quiet inquiry addressed to the room in general.

Dani sized her up before responding. The woman wore a business suit of charcoal-gray, had on sensible shoes, a bulge beneath her jacket that indicated she was armed. She was assessing every individual in the room, almost at once. Her gaze landed on Dani and stuck. "Ms. Sweet?"

Dani stood, ready for anything.

The woman approached. "Tewanda Hardy from the embassy," she said, holding out her hand. "Mercier called." Dani guessed she was really CIA. Their agents often used embassy cover and Mercier had a number of close contacts within the agency. "Our friend, Caterina. How is she?"

Relieved that Mercier had come through with local backup, Dani shook her head. "They're trying to determine that now. She was unconscious when they brought her in."

"Try not to worry," the woman said. "I will be with her while you do what you must. Who is with her now?"

"My partner," Dani said.

Without being asked, Hardy withdrew a flat wallet and handed it to Dani. Her creds identified her as who she claimed to be. Dani handed it back. "Thanks for coming so quickly. You'll call me if there's any change at all in her condition?"

"I have your number and will also be in close contact with Mr. Mercier."

Hardy glanced meaningfully at the restroom down the hallway, then headed for it. Dani followed. There, Hardy took the shoe and gave her items Mercier knew Dani and Ben might need.

They returned to the waiting room and remained silent after that. Dani prayed the blow to Cate's head hadn't done any lasting damage.

Later, as they left the hospital in a taxi, Ben held back the information he had overheard in radiology. Obviously the doctor there assumed that Ben spoke only English. Or perhaps they didn't care one way or the other.

The conversation, held in French-accented German, had been difficult to follow, but Ben had enough of both languages to get the gist of Cate's condition.

"Okay, let's have it," Dani said with a weary sigh. "You're as transparent as glass, Michaels." She sat sort of sideways in the corner of the backseat, looking back toward the hospital. "What did you hear that I didn't?"

He let his shoulders slump and stretched his neck muscles by leaning his head forward and rubbing his nape vigorously. "It looks like a brain stem injury. That's what they're afraid of."

Dani tensed and grabbed his arm. "Oh God, Ben, paralysis?"

"No, no. There's response in her extremities. And she moved on the table. I saw her."

"Then *what?*" Dani asked, again looking out the back window at the gigantic structure where they had left her friend.

"They're worried about…her faculties, I think. I'm not sure. They weren't speaking English, so some of it got past me."

Brain damage. Dani squeezed her eyes shut and cursed. Then she blinked as if to clear her vision.

"Hey, her mind was functioning well when she called out to you in the restaurant after she was hit," Ben reminded Dani. "She made sense. She even told me she never saw the shooter. That was just before she fainted." He took Dani's hand in his. "We have to believe she'll recover, Dani. Don't lose faith."

She nodded, holding his fingers in a death grip.

"So what now? We catch this guy, right?" he said, hoping to distract her through purpose.

"Damn straight," she answered, her voice gruff and just shy of tears. "Now we catch him."

She had given the taxi driver an address that was not for the hotel. Ben figured they must be on the way to that safe house Mercier had arranged. "I'll need my computer," Ben said. "If I can hack into some serious stamp collecting sites, we might get lucky and find out where the deal's going down, if there's any chatter about it on the Web, that is."

"Our things and Cate's have already been picked up," she told him. "We can't go back to the hotel. It's not safe to."

"I need to give that laptop a workout as soon as we get where we're going. We need to get to the bottom of this."

"With a vengeance," she said through gritted teeth.

Yes, vengeance had become the name of the game, Ben thought—now it was working both ways. Dani wanted payback for what had happened to Cate. And Victor Bruegel wanted some serious retribution for a supposed wrong Ben had dòne to him.

Bruegel must hate his guts for some reason, but damned if Ben could figure out why. He had saved the man's life, kept him alive against all odds after the truck bomb.

He wished he had been able to save the others. Their deaths couldn't account for Bruegel's hatred, though. Victor hadn't even liked the family they were transporting to the border.

Besides, how the hell had Victor gained the power to set up an operation like this? Ben hadn't been out of the game *that* long. How had Bruegel gotten control of Persand Inc.?

An even larger mystery was how the man had convinced Kelior and Belken to carry this out. To commit treason. To kill innocents. He sure hadn't generated that much loyalty when he had been under Ben's command.

Greed, of course.

"When I was on the phone with him, Mercier told me they went after Bruegel to bring him in for questioning," Ben said. "He's disappeared. No trace."

"Think he's over here?" she asked.

"I hope so. I'd sure like a little face time with him at this point."

"Maybe he's in the car that's been following us," she said calmly, removing her hand from his. "Wouldn't that be too good to be true?"

Ben turned around and peered out the back of the taxi. "That blue sedan?"

She nodded.

"You plan to let them catch us," he guessed. "Where?"

"At an opportune place, at least for *us*."

She reached in her purse and pulled out a Walther PPK. "Here, take this. Our new pal from the embassy shares her toys." She handed him an extra clip. "Get as close as you can. Take body shots so you won't miss. You any kind of marksman?"

Ben grinned as he examined the pistol and got familiar with the feel of it. "I'll muddle through."

He was ready to mix it up with these goons. Locating stamps had sort of dropped down his priority list.

Chapter 15

Dani poked the driver on the shoulder with her free
hand and dropped a wad of bills on the front seat and
gave him orders in French. "Go left just ahead. Get us
out of the city and show me how fast you can do it."

The cab swerved. The driver sped dangerously
through the traffic.

Ben swayed with the turns and gave a fleeting
thought to his mother. He hoped she was holding up
all right. He should have called today to reassure her,
but he hated to lie to her. How was it moms always
knew about it when you did?

"What's that smile all about?" Dani asked. She

gripped the armrest and braced herself in the corner between the back of the seat and the door.

"I was thinking about my mother," he admitted.

Dani gave a cough of disbelief and rolled her eyes.

"What's wrong with that?" He remembered her past. "You've got issues. Sorry, I forgot."

"*I* have issues?" she asked with a laugh. "You're the mama's boy." She paused, then added, "Benji."

Ben could see how she'd reached that conclusion. He wondered himself at times if he wasn't becoming what she said. He had tried hard not to harbor any resentment about giving up his career. He had made his choice, and for a very good reason. The guilt could get a hell of a lot worse if he stressed his mother to death.

"It nearly killed her before, my coming home in the shape I was in," he told Dani. "At one point, she was closer to death than I was, so excuse me if I take a minute to worry about how the outcome of this might affect her."

"Heart problems?" Dani asked, frowning, feeling a little foolish for teasing him.

He nodded. "And still at risk."

"Hard to believe a mother would expect her son to give up his life for hers."

Ben knew Dani didn't understand. With the only reference to parents that she had, how could she? "She would never ask that, and I didn't give up my life."

Dani's gaze met his. "Didn't you?"

"No!"

"Okay, so stay in one piece and don't give her any more shocks." She sighed. "Then you can get back to your bank."

"That's the plan," he snapped. But what Dani said bothered him. A lot. Would his mother want him to deny what he was, to live the half-life he had chosen now? She had never asked him to give up his career and its element of danger, but Ben realized he sort of blamed her for the existence he had in Ellerton. Just an existence, no movement. Since he had fully recovered, the suit he had put on had begun to chafe.

He shook off the worry for now. He had to survive today and see that Dani did, too. His best chance of doing that required total focus on the problem at hand. He promptly dismissed any thoughts that would distract him during the combat they faced here very shortly.

They were the prey at the moment. "Become the predator," he muttered beneath his breath. A coldness stole over him, as it always did when he went into hunting mode. He was no longer escaping a threat, but luring it to destruction. The weapon warmed in his grasp, became an extension of his arm, his hand, his mind.

Dani met his gaze. Her eyes widened with what appeared to be surprise. Then she gave him an infinitesimal nod of approval.

"Any premonitions I should know about?" he asked, his words almost lost in the screech of tires when their driver left the highway and began bumping down a winding, unpaved road.

Dani shook her head, her attention locked on the path behind them. He thought she might be lying. It didn't matter though. He needed no advance warnings anyway, psychic or otherwise. They had left civilization and entered a wooded area with curves and turns that offered possibilities.

Things were about to get interesting.

Victor Bruegel threw his shaving kit across the room. He clutched the cell phone to his ear and breathed through gritted teeth until he got his temper in hand.

"Where the hell are they *now?*" he demanded, then managed to calm himself a little when Kelior told him that Michaels and the woman were in sight of his men and would soon be history.

He sat on the edge of the bed and glared out the window of the Bahnhof Hotel, imagining that on the city's streets he could see the chase ensuing miles away in the neighboring country. He wished he were there. Wished he could pull the trigger as he looked straight into Ben Michaels's eyes. But he'd have to take what he could get.

"Get rid of them and leave *no* traces, understand? This cannot come back on us."

On *me,* he meant. He didn't give a damn about Kelior.

Kelior had the money, soon to be exchanged for the more portable stamps that he would provide to the al Muhad group.

Every move of the funds had included some incrimination of Michaels. The feds would pick up on that soon.

Victor again told himself he wasn't a traitor; betraying his country wasn't his intent. The money wasn't nearly enough to finance a huge disaster. He couldn't justify backing anything major, even to enrich Persand Inc. But a couple of incidents would jack up the threat level in the U.S. and increase sales considerably. Besides, if he didn't provide funding, they'd get it somewhere else, so it was not *really* enabling the enemy. Business was business.

The funds were a pittance compared to the government contracts he was looking at. Those would get signed and sealed as soon as the al Muhad bunch acted. The group would probably import some bombers, get them wired, hit a mall, maybe a theme park. That ought to do it. Minimal loss. Maximum scare.

But first, he had to make certain Michaels was buried. And that female fed with him. They had no real information connecting things to him or to Persand, Victor was certain. Nothing they could *prove* anyway. He had that covered. But Michaels might somehow guess who had it in for him. Ben always had a sixth sense when it came to figuring things out. Too bad he hadn't used that in Afghanistan when it counted.

Even if Ben never got a clue, Victor wanted him dead and dishonored, even more than he wanted a wildly successful company and more money than he could ever spend. Riches would mean nothing if Michaels was walking around free and happy after what he'd done.

As he spoke, Victor gripped the phone hard enough to bend the thin plastic. "I want him destroyed and I want it *now*," he declared. "*Your* survival is linked directly to the success of that."

He ended the call abruptly. Kelior had things in hand.

The dirt road, little more than a curving, rutted track through the woods, narrowed. The driver had to brake for a sharp turn. Dani ordered the cabbie to stop. As soon as he did, she had the door open. "Go, go!" she shouted to the driver the instant they had cleared the car. She pounded on the fender, then dashed into the brush beside the road. The taxi spun off, slinging dirt and grass, and flew around the next curve. The vehicle disappeared from view, even as she heard the chase car approaching.

"Take cover over there and go for the tires," she ordered, bracing her arm against a large tree to steady her aim. "Do it as soon as we spot the car, before they get even with us so we don't shoot each other! Unless they throw down and surrender, I'll take the driver. You go for the passenger. Ready?"

Ben dropped to a crouch behind a tall pine. The blue Citroen wheeled into view and they opened fire on the tires. The car veered and hit a tree. Doors flew open and men spilled out, already firing. Ben jacked in a fresh clip.

Dani's plan would have worked perfectly if there had been only the driver and passenger. Unfortunately, two more gunmen fled from the backseat into the woods.

Ben got the front seat passenger in the leg. Dani winged the driver as he ran. Two hits, but non-debilitating hits. Ben dropped and rolled across the road, firing into the trees where the men had run.

"Dani?" he called when he reached the tree where she had been but didn't find her there.

They stood a better chance if they were together and could watch each other's backs.

"Here," she rasped, crawling to his side from where she had concealed herself. "You okay?"

He nodded and spoke in a low monotone. "The backseat boys will probably circle around to get behind us. The two we hit are still armed, too. Your guy staggered over that way. Mine is on the ground, using the back wheel for cover. I'm taking them out before the other two get in place and we catch it from both directions. Cover me."

He gave Dani no time to argue, just took off, zig-zagging the twelve to fifteen yards between him and the wrecked sedan. She pumped several rounds beneath the car and more into the trees to cover him. Ben took a chance. He whirled around the back of the vehicle and threw himself on top of the man lying flat on the ground.

They struggled for the weapon he held, an AK-47 that could have cut Ben in two. But he held fast to both the man's wrists and managed a swift kick to his injured leg. With a harsh cry of pain, the shooter went rigid. Ben crowned him with the butt of the captured gun and watched him collapse.

That one act flashed Ben right back to his hospital stay.

"And what did you *feel* when you dealt serious injury or death to someone?" Ben heard the shrink ask him. That holier-than-thou attitude. He had hated the therapy forced on him in the hospital—he had learned too much about himself.

"Safer," he had answered honestly. Not a satisfactory reply, he had found out. But now, right this second, he did feel safer than he had moments ago. And he was about to feel safer still, as soon as he took out the other shooter hiding in the bushes. He knew that one, damn his soul.

He heard the rustle. "Give it up, Kelior," Ben said in a normal tone. "It's over."

In answer to that, two shots chipped bark off the tree inches from Ben's head.

"Okay, your choice," Ben replied. He tossed off another couple of rounds in Kelior's direction. The shots that answered his missed. Hearing rapid clicks, Ben rushed the fallen Kelior before he could reload. He kicked him in the temple. "Two down," he said to himself.

He did a cursory check for other weapons and found a knife strapped to Kelior's leg. He took it, then gathered up the automatics as Dani joined him.

"Impressive," she commented. "Are you *freakin' nuts?*"

"Sometimes," he admitted. That was probably his shrink's conclusion, too. He had let the woman think she'd reprogrammed him, though. For her sake and his mom's. He liked to keep people happy.

"It just irritates the hell out of me to get shot at, even if I shoot first," he grumbled. "Is that really so out of whack?"

Dani chuckled and grabbed the AK-47 from his hands. She plundered the shooter's coat pockets and retrieved the clips. "Well, don't sign up for anger management today. We've still got two more out there."

He touched her lips with his finger. "Be quiet." She stilled immediately, understanding without his having to insist. Ben listened for the approach. He hoped these men weren't well trained. Street thugs generally weren't, and he couldn't imagine who else Kelior could have hired on such short notice.

Then again, maybe they were from one of the cells that had received rigorous military training. Maybe they were as adept at search and destroy as he was.

He didn't hear a thing. Birds had flown. There were no nature noises to mask movement. Maybe the two who had been in the backseat had feared they were surrounded and just...ran.

And maybe there was a Santa after all.

"They didn't circle. They're staked out down the road, waiting," Dani said. "That's the only way out of here. They'll take us as we go back."

"You sure?"

She nodded.

"Rom certain?" He raised his eyebrows and smiled, his bottom lip caught between his perfect white teeth.

Dani bobbed her head once as she grinned back at him, obviously amused by the term he had just coined and probably surprised that he would tease her about her Gypsy gift.

She dropped to one knee and fished around in her shoulder purse. Activating her phone, she punched in a number from the list Cate had given her. "Resources," she explained. "We have no transportation

Special Agent's Seduction

back to town." She checked her watch again, gave their coordinates off her GPS readout and ordered them a ride.

"What about the two waiting for us down the road?"

She smiled and checked her watch again. "Oh, we'll have them secured by the time a car gets out here, don't you think?"

He smiled back.

"No sense sitting around waiting. Let's check out the car, get these guys tied up and go." God, Dani was a girl after his own heart. No pretense about her, nothing false. No weakness, either. She didn't like violence any better than he did, but she would damn well dish it out before she took it.

Now that seemed like fairly sane programming to him.

Ben suffered a brief epiphany in that moment, realizing that he had indulged in pretense, falseness, and, yeah, a little weakness this past year. Even if he looked totally different than before, he hadn't changed inside. He was still a soldier.

He joined Dani as they quickly searched the damaged car for money, stamps and anything else incriminating to add to the illegal automatic weapons the occupants had brought along.

"Nothing! What the hell did he *do* with it?" Ben growled. He fished in the corner of the trunk and came up with a coil of thin cable and a pair of wire cutters.

"How far down the road are they?" he asked, grunting with effort as he rolled the unconscious Kelior over to tie him with a length of the cable.

"Far enough," she said, putting the finishing touches on her shooter's bonds. "How's your guy doing? Mine has a flesh wound in the upper thigh. Stopped bleeding," she said, wiping one hand on the nearby grass.

Ben looked down at Kelior and plucked at the sleeve covering the spot were Dani had winged him. "Still out like a light, but he'll live. How're you fixed for ammo?"

"Good to go," she said, sliding back the carriage on her pistol and peering down the sight. She tucked it in her holster and took up the AK.

"Me, too." Ben pointed to the opposite side of the road. "Stay well back, move slowly and keep your ears trained. Soon as you hear or spot them, close in, but keep at least ten yards back this side of them to avoid crossfire." He delivered a pointed look along with the same patronizing warning she had given him earlier.

"Touché," she said, wrinkling her nose at him. "By the way, you know I'll have to identify myself, offer them a chance to give up. No tires to shoot out this time."

Ben groaned. "This is combat, Dani. They're not going to throw down. We'll lose the element of surprise."

"Sorry. Rules," she said.

"Have it your way. I'll give you a bird call when I'm in place. Wait for it."

She laughed, heading out through the bushes on her side of the road. "That is so *hokey*. Like that won't alert them?"

He shrugged. "So they'll be alert. Besides, you're warning them first. You clearly love a challenge."

She moved out of sight then, working her way parallel to the road, just as he did on the opposite side.

Adrenaline rushed through his veins along with an energy he welcomed. He had felt more alive these past few days than he had since before he'd been wounded. It was like coming out of a fugue state. Dani had brought him back to life in other ways, too. Hell, he hadn't even had a date, hadn't kissed a woman, hadn't thought about sex in over a year. He grimaced. Okay, he had thought about sex. A lot, actually. But the urgency had been missing. At one point he rationalized that he had probably had his share and someone else's, too, before age thirty, and that he'd rather do without it than deal with the consequences.

In a small town like Ellerton where everybody knew everybody and everything that went on, there were *always* consequences. None of those had appealed to him.

As it happened, there were consequences to hooking up with Dani, too: he wanted her, and not just temporarily. This need for some kind of permanent commitment between them was the main consequence he had to deal with. Could she handle that?

He glanced in her direction, relieved when he saw no sign of her and heard nothing. Yeah, Dani could handle anything, he thought with pride. A girl after his own heart, all right. And he was definitely going to be the guy after hers.

A sharp trilling bird whistle yanked his attention back to business. Damn, she had beaten him to the punch. Would she wait for him to answer?

He heard a mumble of voices and click of weapons being cocked. Ben crept closer to the road, spied the quarry and zeroed in on the one with the biggest gun. They would open fire the instant Dani yelled to identify herself. He couldn't let that happen.

"*Rendez vos armes!* Surrender your weapons!" he thundered, then dropped flat on the ground. Good thing. A steady barrage of bullets cracked into trees all around him. One buzzed past his ear like an angry insect.

He scrambled sideways and took cover behind a stout hemlock. Peering around it when the firing ceased, he saw Dani emerge onto the road, the AK-47 trained on the two men writhing on the ground, both clutching their legs.

Ben joined her and gathered up the abandoned weaponry, stacking it safely to one side. "Excellent shooting," he said, inclining his head to the targets. He could see she was mad.

"You were protecting me, drawing their fire," she accused.

"Yeah, well…it was a wild impulse."

She didn't comment. The distant yodel of sirens told him her silent treatment wouldn't last long. If he knew Dani, she would have her say before company got in the way.

Then she glanced at him, just a brief flick of her head in his direction. As their eyes met, Dani muttered the dead-last thing he would have expected. "Thanks."

And then she smiled.

The local cops arrived, along with two ambulances. Dani phoned Mercier while the paramedics dealt with wounds and loaded the shooters into the waiting vehicles. She and Ben rode back with the police who would be escorting the four prisoners through further treatment at the hospital.

"Mercier's sending backup. He says they traced Bruegel to Frankfurt, where he disappeared again. He could be on the run if he suspects we're on to him, or headed this way to handle the stamp deal himself." She sounded very official. All government agent. Even *that* turned him on.

She had thanked him for putting her safety first. Deep down, he wanted her to *really* thank him for caring, to take him to her bed and keep him there, touching, loving, belonging.

Not likely to happen. Dani Sweet was too freaking independent. She didn't need any man.

If she could only love and want him, that would be enough. But she didn't *need* him.

She was focused on the job and he should be, too. "We need to interrogate Kelior as soon as possible. If you want to go ahead and see about Cate, I can do that."

"I figure they'll have to sedate him. It will probably be morning before we can get any answers." Dani shoved her hands through her hair and shook her head as if to clear it. She took a deep breath and released it slowly. "I need to be the one to question him."

"Don't you have a rule about waiting until he's lucid?" Ben asked.

Dani took her time considering what he said. "I'll have to wait until he can understand his rights or nothing he says will be admissible in court."

Ben shrugged. "Nothing says *I* have to wait. Maybe it's monkeying with the rules, but I'm not restricted by a badge. I'm just the pissed-off banker trying to get his money back."

"The local police don't know that," Dani reminded him. "You've been riding on my creds. They think you're my partner."

"Goes to show you how dangerous it is to assume things."

"No, I'm sorry, Ben. I can't let you do it. End of discussion."

"Okay," he replied. No need to discuss it any further.

They arrived at the hospital shortly after the ambulances and watched the men get off-loaded and wheeled through to the emergency treatment area with well-armed, uniformed police flanking the gurneys.

Ben reached for her hand when she started in after the last gurney cleared the door. "Wait a minute," he said, drawing her to one side, out of the way of the ER traffic.

"What?" She looked up at him, her hand clinging to his. He expected impatience, which would have been justified. They had work to do here. Instead he saw exhaustion and a need to be held.

The adrenaline rush that had carried her through this far had waned. He knew the feeling. With his free hand, he cupped her chin. He let his fingers trace the line of her jaw, then rest there, just touching for the sake of touching. She closed her eyes and leaned into the caress.

Ben took a deep breath and threw caution to the winds. What was the worst she could say? The next few hours would be a whirlwind. More of her team would be here by morning to replace Cate and to assist with the investigation now that there were suspects in custody. He might not get her alone again.

"Will you stay with me tonight? After you see about Cate? After we've finished with Kelior and the others?"

Her fingers threaded through his and she sighed. "Ben, you know that's a bad idea." She shook her head, but it looked to him more like regret than an outright refusal.

"Is that a no?" he asked, to make certain.

She looked confused and maybe even a little desperate. He let go of her hand when she tugged on it.

He watched her turn away from him, then look back over her shoulder. "No," she said, the word clipped. Her lips pressed together, then parted again as she added, "No, that's not a no."

Ben smiled. But she was already gone, whisking through the doorway to the emergency room.

Chapter 16

Ben finished with Kelior in record time. The man was so goofy on morphine, he spilled everything. But Kelior's confession was disjointed. Pieces were missing.

"Did you check on Cate?" he asked Dani as he joined her in the hallway.

"What were you doing in Kelior's room?" she demanded in a gruff whisper.

"Nothing that will impede your investigation or prosecution," he assured her.

"I ought to arrest *you!*" she snapped.

"Do what you have to," he said. "But first, how's Cate?"

"She's awake and grousing about the hotel's lack of security and the fact that she never got dinner. Apart from horrible dizziness and the expected pain in her shoulder, she seemed okay. She insisted I carry on. So, what did you find out?"

"Kelior was definitely in it to set me up," Ben told her. "And for his cut, of course." He slugged down the cup of coffee she handed him, excellent brew for hospital fare. "Belken's just muscle. He was in it for the money."

"You think Kelior was holding something back, don't you?"

She had not yet gone into the darkened room where Kelior was isolated, cuffed to a hospital bed and hooked up to an IV and monitoring equipment. The police guarding his door never offered any objection to Ben's questioning the prisoner.

"In his condition, I expect he's giving me all he knows," Ben answered. "Bruegel told him that I tried to finger him as a Taliban agent. He also thinks I set his mother up to be killed. Bruegel told him I had been manufacturing proof against him. Apparently, Kelior believed I was still determined to continue that after I got well enough to pursue it again."

"You think he really is an agent?" Dani asked.

"No, if there had been any question of that, he

would never have been allowed to go on the Afghan mission in the first place. He admitted that he, Belken and some guy named Terrence planned the bank job. This Terrence, whoever he is, supplied the account numbers and the gunman."

"One with Middle Eastern looks and accent. Interesting," Dani said. "Wonder whose idea that was."

Ben continued. "Bruegel's. Kelior acted as lookout while Belken waited in the Caymans to collect their share and forward the rest on to the Swiss bank as this Terrence had ordered."

"So, like we figured, Bruegel called Belken in Grand Cayman from Ellerton to tell him you were alive and on the way, and also to get rid of you," Dani said, sipping her coffee and grimacing as they rode the elevator down to the ground floor. "It was Belken on the boat."

"Right, along with a hired gun. He did contact Kelior by satellite phone after the boat flipped, so he survived, at least long enough to do that. I guess if he managed to call Kelior, he could have gotten in touch with someone in Grand Cayman to rescue him, but Kelior hasn't heard from him since."

"You think their cut of the money went down with Belken in the boat?"

"That's what Kelior's afraid happened. Anyway, that call was how Kelior was able to reach Toronto in time to get the bomb on our plane. He waited around, found out we survived that, too, and flew straight here. He beat us by a couple of hours, thanks to our layover in Iceland."

"Wonder how he found three little helpers so fast."

Ben shrugged. "Kelior's father's from Greece. So are these guys. What Bruegel told Kelior made him damned desperate to get rid of me. But he had no clue who you were or that the feds were even involved."

"So where's the rest of the money?"

"Kelior didn't say before the morphine put him under. We'll question him again in the morning. I want to get back into the Persand site and take another look at their personnel files. Maybe we can find this Terrence guy."

Dani smiled ruefully. "You're going to be really busy the rest of the night."

He headed for the nearest cab parked just beyond the hospital doors. "Get in. You're about to see the speediest hacking job in the history of computers."

The black cab upholstery smelled of expensive cologne and cigarette smoke. The driver sat still, his gloved hand flexing on the wheel, awaiting instructions.

Through the interior window Dani provided him an address adjacent to the safe house where their gear was now stowed. She regretted that they weren't going back to their rooms at the Bellevue Palace hotel. There would be at least two other agents at the safe house. She needed to be alone with Ben.

Ben slid in beside her, moving her purse from between them so they could sit close. He fastened her seat belt for her, then quickly did his own. His gaze locked on hers. "At last," he muttered, the words crushed between his mouth and hers.

Dani didn't deny herself the pleasure of his kiss. What was the point? There wouldn't be any privacy for it later.

His tongue traced her lips, exciting nerves there that triggered immediate arousal. She loved his mouth.

His palm glided over her waist, around to her back, fingers slipping just inside the waistband of her slacks to rub the indentation of her spine. She loved his hands. His touch.

A sigh billowed through her as she snuggled closer, ignoring the cut of the seat belt, not even minding the obstruction of shoulder holster and weapon.

He broke the kiss, laughed a little at his own breathlessness, and gave her waist a fond squeeze. "Sorry, got carried away."

"Me, too," she admitted in a whisper. He cut off the words with another heady kiss. She didn't mind at all. She loved his kiss.

She loved *him*. The realization hit her all at once, though she grew still and stopped reciprocating. The truth scared her.

How long had she known this man? Less than three days? And yet, she seemed to know him better than she had her two previous lovers, even after months of dating and actually living with them.

He must have noticed her lack of enthusiasm. "What is it?" he asked, his mouth only a fraction of an inch away, his words tickling as he spoke them.

"N-nothing," she answered, seeking his mouth again. But he avoided the kiss.

She took a breath and ran her tongue over her lips, savoring his taste. He didn't love her. Couldn't. How could anyone be expected to fall as fast and hard as she had? It was incredible. And frightening.

"Something's wrong," he said softly. "Tell me."

Dani didn't know what to say. She could hardly admit the truth. He would probably laugh out loud. And probably run like hell as soon as he could get away. She braced a hand on his chest and pushed back. "Too much, too soon," she said with a breathless little laugh.

"Oh." He looked around, as if noticing for the first time that they were stuck in the backseat of a weird-smelling taxi, doing forty miles per hour down a dark alley.

"An alley?" She tensed just as he did. The taxi slammed on brakes and the lights went off, pitching them into total darkness. No streetlights. No dash lights. Nothing.

"I have NVGs and can see you clearly. Toss your weapons in the front seat," the cabbie commanded. "Or I *will* kill you."

By this time, Dani already had her pistol in her hand, safety off. She could fire through the back of the driver's seat, but he could still get a shot off. Several, even if his gun wasn't an automatic. He would be dead, but so would they. At this range he couldn't possibly miss, even without night-vision goggles.

She felt Ben release her seat belt and heard the click of his as he reached over and dropped something—his borrowed weapon, she supposed—into the front passenger seat.

"Victor," he said as he did that. "I wondered when you'd say hello."

The driver laughed. "Did you? You'll forgive me if I don't shake hands." He cleared his throat and Dani sensed a movement. She could smell gun oil very close to her nose. "Get rid of your weapon, honey, or I will blow you away."

"Go ahead, Dani," Ben murmured. "Do as he says."

Never give up your weapon. Never. Her instructor's voice filled her head, demanding she stick to her training. But she had no choice. Dani reached over carefully and dropped her H&K into the front seat.

She had a backup in her purse if she could only get to it. Unfortunately, the purse was on the other side of Ben. And even if she had the little .22 in her hand right this minute, she wouldn't be any better off than she had been with the H&K.

"What's the plan now, Victor?" Ben asked, his voice just shy of taunting. "You know the feds are after you, right?"

Bruegel laughed. "You always did underestimate your men, Michaels. How stupid do you think I am? There's not a shred of evidence that I had anything to do with this."

"There is now," Ben argued. "We have Kelior and he's been singing like a canary in heat."

"No good," Victor said, a smile in his voice. "All I did was make him aware that you had it in for him. That you were the one who had his mother killed last year when she was on a shopping trip to Paris. He's convinced you were undercover instead of recovering."

"Why, Victor? What have I ever done to you? I saved your worthless hide after that truck blew up."

The ensuing silence lasted several seconds. The vehicle seemed to become dense with a sense of loathing. She could hear Bruegel's harsh breathing as he tried to bring his fury under control. "That's just it. You *saved* me. And for what, Michaels? So I could walk around on an aluminum leg? No woman will so much as look at me now."

"They weren't all that interested *before,* if I recall. So you resort to treason, Victor? Because of a missing leg? Why didn't you just come after me?"

"If you hadn't insisted on dragging that damned family to the border, I'd have come home whole. You *are* a traitor and I mean to see you branded one if it's the last thing I do. You put that damn Pashti *schoolteacher* and his brats ahead of *us,* your own American men!"

Ben said nothing in his defense.

Bruegel's words came faster, spitting with venom. "But you. You had the best, didn't you? Face rebuilt—even better than before. Injuries all healed. You don't deserve to live, much less live the way you do!"

"You've done pretty well for yourself," Ben reminded him. "CEO of Persand. How'd you luck into that? Kill somebody?"

Bruegel gave a satisfied little grunt. "As a matter of fact, yes. My new boss. And he was kind enough to change his will first. I inherited his sixty-seven percent share of the company stock. With a little encouragement, of course."

"So now you kill us and go your merry way?" Ben asked. "She's a fed, Victor. They'll hunt you down like a rabid dog and you'll never even see a trial."

Victor laughed. "That's supposed to dissuade me, Ben?"

"You want to die, Victor? I'll kill you right now."

The laughter grew wilder and a little more distant. He had thrown his head back. A bright light suddenly flashed, nearly blinding Dani and certainly blinding the man wearing NVGs.

Dani ducked as far down as she could, expecting shots, but Ben was half over the seat, struggling with Bruegel. Suddenly the fight stopped. The flashlight, probably the one she carried in her purse, had rolled into the floorboard and cast an eerie glow over the interior.

Ben hung over the seat, his body tense as strung wire. A choking sound emerged from near the steering wheel. A last gasp and there was only the rapid breathing of her and Ben.

"Is he dead?" she whispered.

"I think," Ben said, shifting his weight. "I feel a pulse, but it's probably mine."

Dani opened the car door, flooding the vehicle with light. Ben had one large hand clutched around Victor's throat and the other pressing Victor's right wrist to the car seat. The pistol hung from his trigger finger.

Dani snatched the gun away and quickly ran around and retrieved theirs from the front passenger seat. "All clear unless he has a backup," she said. "I'll search him."

"Don't touch him," Ben warned. "Stay back."

Dani walked around, yanked open the driver's door and crowned Bruegel on the temple, a knockout blow if she had ever dealt one, if he had been conscious to begin with. "You can let go now. We'll let a coroner check for signs of life."

Ben slumped back, released a harsh breath of relief and flexed his hand. "Thanks."

"You're welcome," she said with a sigh. "Let's put him in the boot and go wind this up. I'm ready to go home."

"We still don't have the money," Ben argued as he pulled Victor from behind the wheel and dragged him to the back of the car. Dani grabbed the keys from the ignition and opened the trunk, hoping to find something with which to bind Bruegel.

"Uh-oh," she said, but it was more in the way of surprise than warning.

"What is it?" Ben huffed as he dropped Victor on the ground. "The real cabbie in there?"

Dani nodded and pointed the little flashlight at the body.

Ben stuffed his clothes into his bag, cursing foully when it wouldn't zip shut. His mood had degenerated in direct proportion to how little he had seen of Dani since the taxi incident. Not once alone. Mercier was keeping her busy. Ben had gone back to the hotel to catch a few hours' sleep. It was midmorning and past the hour he should have checked out.

Bruegel had obviously gotten the money from Kelior's room before he'd come after them. Kelior's and Belken's share lay somewhere on the ocean floor along with Ace and his pal. Insurance would cover that portion.

The fact that Bruegel was still breathing didn't sit well with Ben. He didn't like to kill, but that one seriously needed to expire. The man *wanted* to die, too, that was the thing.

Someone tapped on his door. Probably the maid.

When he opened the door, Dani stood there, beautifully decked out in a fitted brown jacket of raw silk, unbuttoned to show a slinky yellow top and a beige skirt that reached nearly to her ankles.

"Classy," he commented, noting the lack of a shoulder holster. Made him wonder what was under the skirt.

"Thanks." Her suede, high-heeled boots clicked on the entry tiles as she brushed past him. "Jack said you were flying out commercial." Her amber eyes sparkled. Tears?

Ben hoped she was sad about parting company. He was damn near devastated. He hadn't been able to face a flight back with her whole team, where he'd have to sit there and share her. Cate, Mercier, Vanessa Senate and their new guy, Jake Radford. Every one of them had some kind of psychic talent, Cate had said. Fine deal that would be. They'd have him pegged as a heartsick loser before the plane got off the ground.

Okay, he might *be* that, but he didn't like to advertise. And he especially didn't want Dani to know. She probably wouldn't be able to tell, since her trick was premonitions.

"Too much, too fast, huh?" he muttered under his breath as he closed the door. How the devil was he supposed to go slowly when they lived two hundred miles apart? She hadn't suggested he do that anyway. Her recent avoidance pretty much indicated he should leave her alone.

"I could drive up to McLean the end of next week," he said. That had come totally out of the blue. He had not intended to say anything remotely like that. Now she'd shoot him down again. Man, was he a glutton for punishment.

"No," she said, just as he predicted. Hell, maybe he was into premonitions, too. Then she glanced at him sideways and smiled a secret smile. "I won't be there."

"Oh…okay then. Just a thought." A wish, a hope, a prayer. All shot down in flames.

She sashayed over to the window, her skirt swinging around her legs, enticing his gaze to follow the motion. With one hand, she parted the curtains and looked out. "Switzerland's nice, but you know, I like Iceland better. Romantic. All that steam. Great place to make love."

Ben's heart raced. She glanced at him over her shoulder in that way she had. "Want to come?"

"Now there's a loaded question."

She laughed with him as she turned and walked straight into his waiting arms. "You love me." Then she rose on her toes and kissed him.

Ben could have conquered the world in that moment. "You sound very sure of yourself," he teased.

"Rom certain," she replied, sliding her arms around his waist. "We know these things. Like, I *know* I love you. In all your incarnations…uptight banker…hard fighting soldier…tireless lover. You continue to confuse me, but I don't care anymore."

"And how did you come to this conclusion after fighting it so hard?" Ben asked, truly interested in what turned her around.

She closed her eyes and exhaled, her fingers toying with his shirt, untucking it in back. "Well, I did a lot of soul searching." She opened her eyes and peered into his. "I don't think I can live without you, whoever you are."

He kissed her again, his own soul filled with gratitude and determination to make her happy, whatever it took. "We'll go slow," he promised. "I won't ask you for any life-altering decisions until at least next week."

"There will be problems to work out, Ben. Our jobs. Logistics. Your family, if they have objections. So, no mentioning the *M* word for at least six months," she warned. "We have to get better acquainted." She slid her hand under the front of his shirt and tickled his chest, playfully at first, then smoothed her palm over his heart, absorbing its beat. She grinned. "But the *L* word is okay."

"I love you," he said sincerely. "But you know that. Must be nice to have friends who read minds for you."

"It does help. Eliminates the risk of rejection," she admitted. "But I'll take my premonitions any day of the week."

He embraced her fully and rested his chin on the top of her head, feeling every inch of her pressed against him, just as she should be. "So where do you see us in, say, half an hour from now?"

"Together somewhere soft and pillowy. Like that bed over there."

"And years from now?" he asked seriously, threading his fingers through her hair and holding her so that he could see her eyes sparkle again.

She shrugged. "Together. Forever. It's all I *can* see."

He gazed deeply into the amber Gypsy eyes that held his future. "I see that, too. It's really all we need to know."

Epilogue

"Doesn't Ben look handsome in his dress blues?" his mother crooned. "Bless his heart, he never wanted to be anything but a soldier." She shook her head and smiled fondly. "He hated banking. Now he'll be happier, working in the Pentagon."

"You're okay with it, Mrs. Michaels?" Cate asked, offering the groom's mother a tissue when a tear trailed down her powdered cheek. "Ben was worried that his going back on duty might upset you."

"Oh, it *did,* honey! You know he was almost killed once." She daubed at her eyes, her gaze never leaving her son who stood tall at the altar, his father beside him as best man. Cate had volunteered to keep the mother of the groom company in her pew. "But I don't have to worry anymore. Danielle will look after him. She's *prescient,* you know."

"Prescient?" Cate almost laughed. Dani had been so anxious about Ben's parents accepting her as a daughter-in-law.

"That means *prophetic.* She can actually see the future!" Mrs. Michaels whispered, shivering with excitement. "She's a Gypsy. First one I ever met. Except for her sister, but we never knew Carol was. I was just floored when Ben told us! In a *good* way, though."

Cate managed to look surprised. "Floored, huh?"

But Mrs. Michaels didn't hear. She was looking back down the aisle now, as the organist played the chords announcing the bride's entrance. "Oh, *look!*" She sighed as fresh tears gathered. "There's our new daughter. Isn't she darling?"

Cate almost snickered. No one but Ben and his parents would ever describe Dani as a darling. She was a hard-hitting, straight-shooting, hyperactive pain in the butt most of the time. Ben would have his hands full. And God help them both if their offspring inherited their combined strong wills and daring.

Well, maybe Dani did look darling in her simple ecru-satin gown, Cate thought. The veil of matching lace was elegance itself. She was also wearing that bridelike, wistful look as she spied Ben waiting for her in front of the pulpit. Love like theirs was about as pure and undiluted as it came.

The service at the Ellerby United Methodist was over in less than twenty minutes, ending with a kiss that threatened to set the altar cloth on fire. The organist struck several chords again, until they broke their embrace. Dani and Ben turned to face their friends and relatives as man and wife.

The sun shining through gorgeous stained-glass windows, the beauty of the couple done up in their wedding finery and the sheer wave of collective happiness in the place were enough to make even Cate weep a little. She sniffed, then laughed.

Ah, weddings were such fun when they weren't hers!

* * * * *

Silhouette® Romantic Suspense
keeps getting hotter!
Turn the page for a sneak preview of the first book
in Marie Ferrarella's latest miniseries
THE DOCTORS PULASKI

HER LAWMAN ON CALL
by Marie Ferrarella

On sale February 2007 wherever books are sold.

Chapter 1

There was something about a parking structure that always made her feel vulnerable. In broad daylight she found them confusing, and most of the time she had too many other things on her mind. Squeezing in that extra piece of information about where she had left her vehicle sometimes created a mental meltdown.

At night, when there were fewer vehicles housed within this particular parking garage, she felt exposed, helpless. And feelings of déjà vu haunted her. It was a completely irrational reaction and as a physician, she was the first to acknowledge this. But still…

Wanting to run, she moved slowly. She retraced

steps she'd taken thirteen hours ago when her day at Patience Memorial Hospital had begun. The lighting down on this level was poor, as one of the bulbs was out, and the air felt heavy and clammy, much like the day had been. Typical New York City early-autumn weather, she thought. She picked up her pace, making her way toward where she thought she remembered leaving her car, a small, vintage Toyota.

Dr. Sasha Pulaski stripped off her sweater and slung it over her arm, stifling a yawn. The sound of her heels echoed back to her. If she was lucky, she could be sound asleep in less than an hour. Never mind food, she thought. All she wanted was to commune with her pillow and a flat surface—any flat surface—for about six hours.

Not too much to ask, she thought. Unless you were an intern. Mercifully, those days were behind her, but still in front of her two youngest sisters. Five doctors and almost-doctors in one family. Not bad for the offspring of two struggling immigrants who had come into this country with nothing more than the clothes on their backs. She knew that her parents were both proud enough to burst.

A strange, popping noise sounded in the distance. Instantly Sasha stiffened, listening. Holding her breath. Memories suddenly assaulted her.

One hand was clenched at her side, and the other held tightly to the purse strap slung over her shoulder. She willed herself to relax. More than likely, it was just someone from the hospital getting into his car and going home. Or maybe it was one of the security guards, accidentally stepping on something on the ground.

In the past six months, several people had been robbed in and around the structure, and as a result the hospital had beefed up security. There was supposed to be at least one guard making the rounds at all times. That didn't make her feel all that safe. The hairs at the back of her neck stood at attention.

As she rounded the corner, heading toward where she might have left her vehicle, Sasha dug into her purse. Not for her keys, but for the comforting cylindrical shape of the small can of mace her father, Josef Pulaski, a retired NYPD police officer, insisted that she and her sisters carry with them at all times. Her fingers tightened around the small dispenser just as she saw a short, squat man up ahead. He had a mop of white hair, a kindly face and, even in his uniform, looked as if he could be a stand-in for a mall Santa Claus.

The security guard, she thought in relief, her fingers growing lax. She'd seen him around and even exchanged a few words with him on occasion. He was retired, with no family. Being a guard gave him something to do, a reason to get up each day.

The next moment, her relief began to slip away. The guard was looking down at something on the ground. There was a deep frown on his face and his body was rigid, as if frozen in place.

Sasha picked up her pace. "Mr. Stevens?" she called out. "Is something wrong?"

His head jerked in her direction. He seemed startled to see her. Or was that horror on his face?

Before she could ask him any more questions, Sasha saw what had robbed him of his speech. There was the body of a woman lying beside a car. Blood pooled beneath her head, streaming toward her frayed tan trench coat. A look of surprise was forever frozen on her pretty, bronze features.

Recognition was immediate. A scream, wide and thick, lodged itself in Sasha's throat as she struggled not to release it.

Angela. One of her colleagues.

She'd talked to Angela a little more than two hours ago. Terror vibrated through Sasha's very being.

How?

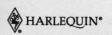

This February…

Catch NASCAR Superstar *Carl Edwards* in

SPEED DATING!

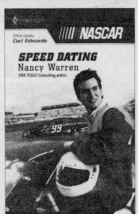

Kendall assesses risk for a living—so she's the last person you'd expect to see on the arm of a race-car driver who thrives on the unpredictable. But when a bizarre turn of events—and NASCAR hotshot Dylan Hargreave—inspire her to trade in her ever-so-structured existence for "life in the fast lane" she starts to feel she might be on to something!

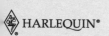

EVERLASTING LOVE™

Every great love has a story to tell ™

Save $1.⁰⁰ off

the purchase of any Harlequin Everlasting Love novel

Coupon valid from January 1, 2007 until April 30, 2007.

Valid at retail outlets in the U.S. only. Limit one coupon per customer.

RETAILER: Harlequin Enterprises Limited will pay the face value of this coupon plus 8¢ if submitted by the customer for this product only. Any other use constitutes fraud. Coupon is nonassignable. Void if taxed, prohibited or restricted by law. Consumer must pay any government taxes. Void if copied. For reimbursement submit coupons and proof of sales directly to: Harlequin Enterprises Ltd., P.O. Box 880478, El Paso, TX 88588-0478, U.S.A. Cash value 1/100¢. Valid in the U.S. only. ® is a trademark of Harlequin Enterprises Ltd. Trademarks marked with ® are registered in the United States and/or other countries.

5 65373 00076 2   (8100) 0 11302

HEUSCPN0407

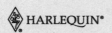

HARLEQUIN®

EVERLASTING LOVE™

Every great love has a story to tell™

Save $1.⁰⁰ off

the purchase of
any Harlequin
Everlasting Love novel

Coupon valid from January 1, 2007
until April 30, 2007.

Valid at retail outlets in Canada only.
Limit one coupon per customer.

52607370

HECDNCPN0407

HARLEQUIN® Romance®

What a month!

In February watch for

Rancher and Protector

Part of the Western Weddings miniseries

BY JUDY CHRISTENBERRY

The Boss's Pregnancy Proposal

BY RAYE MORGAN

Also in February, expect
MORE of what you love
as the Harlequin Romance line
increases to six titles per month.

SRJAN07

REQUEST YOUR FREE BOOKS!

2 FREE NOVELS PLUS 2 FREE GIFTS!

Silhouette® Romantic

SUSPENSE

Sparked by Danger, Fueled by Passion!

YES! Please send me 2 FREE Silhouette® Romantic Suspense novels and my 2 FREE gifts. After receiving them, if I don't wish to receive any more books, I can return the shipping statement marked "cancel." If I don't cancel, I will receive 4 brand-new novels every month and be billed just $4.24 per book in the U.S., or $4.99 per book in Canada, plus 25¢ shipping and handling per book plus applicable taxes, if any*. That's a savings of at least 15% off the cover price! I understand that accepting the 2 free books and gifts places me under no obligation to buy anything. I can always return a shipment and cancel at any time. Even if I never buy another book from Silhouette, the two free books and gifts are mine to keep forever.

240 SDN EEX6   340 SDN EEYJ

Name	(PLEASE PRINT)	
Address		Apt. #
City	State/Prov.	Zip/Postal Code

Signature (if under 18, a parent or guardian must sign)

Mail to the Silhouette Reader Service™:
IN U.S.A.: P.O. Box 1867, Buffalo, NY 14240-1867
IN CANADA: P.O. Box 609, Fort Erie, Ontario L2A 5X3

Not valid to current Silhouette Intimate Moments subscribers.

Want to try two free books from another line?
Call 1-800-873-8635 or visit www.morefreebooks.com.

* Terms and prices subject to change without notice. NY residents add applicable sales tax. Canadian residents will be charged applicable provincial taxes and GST. This offer is limited to one order per household. All orders subject to approval. Credit or debit balances in a customer's account(s) may be offset by any other outstanding balance owed by or to the customer. Please allow 4 to 6 weeks for delivery.

Your Privacy: Silhouette is committed to protecting your privacy. Our Privacy Policy is available online at www.eHarlequin.com or upon request from the Reader Service. From time to time we make our lists of customers available to reputable firms who may have a product or service of interest to you. If you would prefer we not share your name and address, please check here. ☐

SRS07

Silhouette®

COMING NEXT MONTH

INTIMATE MOMENTS™